A Home Subscription! It's the easiest and most convenient way to get every one of the exciting Coventry Romance Novels! ...And you get 4 of them FREE!

You pay nothing extra for this convenience: there are no additional charges...you don't even pay for postage! Fill out and send us the handy coupon now, and we'll send you 4 exciting Coventry Romance novels absolutely FREE!

SEND NO MONEY, GET THESE
FOUR BOOKS
FREE!

C1280

MAIL THIS COUPON TODAY TO:
COVENTRY HOME
SUBSCRIPTION SERVICE
6 COMMERCIAL STREET
HICKSVILLE, NEW YORK 11801

YES, please start a Coventry Romance Home Subscription in my name, and send me FREE and without obligation to buy, my 4 Coventry Romances If you do not hear from me after I have examined my 4 FREE books, please send me the 6 new Coventry Romances each month as soon as they come off the presses. I understand that I will be billed only $10.50 for all 6 books There are no shipping and handling nor any other hidden charges. There is no minimum number of monthly purchases that I have to make In fact, I can cancel my subscription at any time The first 4 FREE books are mine to keep as a gift, even if I do not buy any additional books.

For added convenience, your monthly subscription may be charged automatically to your credit card.

☐ Master Charge   ☐ Visa

Credit Card # _____

Expiration Date _____

Name _____
(Please Print)

Address _____

City _____ State _____ Zip _____

Signature _____

☐ Bill Me Direct Each Month

This offer expires March 31, 1981. Prices subject to change without notice Publisher reserves the right to substitute alternate FREE books. Sales tax collected where required by law. Offer valid for new members only.

THE PLIGHT OF
PAMELA POLLWORTH

Margaret SeBastian

FAWCETT COVENTRY • NEW YORK

THE PLIGHT OF PAMELA POLLWORTH

Published by Fawcett Coventry Books, a unit of CBS Publications, the Consumer Publishing Division of CBS Inc.

ISBN: 0-449-50119-1

Printed in the United States of America

First Fawcett Coventry printing: December 1980

10 9 8 7 6 5 4 3 2 1

To the Chefs of the University at Oxford

and to

HELEN WORTH

Director of

New York City's Helen Worth Cooking School

For the inspiration and background.

Chapter I

It was stifling hot in the heavily-draped, little sitting room, but its occupants, four young ladies, did not seem to mind it. In fact, they were seated as close as was possible before the coal-fire in the grate on the hearth, and all of them had woolen shawls wrapped about their shoulders.

"I tell you never in my life have I been so cold!" exclaimed the Honorable Margery Dawley, pulling her shawl closer about her. "I do declare the very thought of it makes me shudder!"

Apparently she was thinking about it at that very moment, because her shoulders gave a little shake as she spoke.

"Papa says that never in all his days can he recall when London has been as cold," declared the Honorable Pamela Pollworth. "We were in the greatest peril of being left without a single lump of coal. I swear I do not know what we should have done—and the water—"

"Oh, the water!" cried the Honorable Eleanor Fairchild. "I tell you it was merciless! To have to break the ice in the bowl before one could gain the least bit of moisture for one's face—if one had the hardihood—"

"Did you hear that the *Thames* was frozen over?" asked the Honorable Henrietta Blandish, her eyes wide with horror at the thought.

With a superior little laugh, Miss Fairchild remarked: "I should think everyone knows that—and it is a nine-days-wonder, too. My brother Kevin has been out upon the ice and he brought back such tales it is beyond belief. There are *people out upon the ice* of the Thames! Can you believe it?"

"It is more than just people, Eleanor. It is a veritable fair," said Miss Pollworth, the hostess. "Geoffrey says that the newspapers are referring to it as the 'Frost Fair,' and all manner of amusements and entertainments are being conducted right out upon the ice. They have set up shelters of rags and wood and are even cooking over fires built right upon the ice. He thinks it is a bang-up go and has been out to see it every day—"

Miss Dawley turned pink and tittered. "Oh, Pam! How you talk! It is such an unladylike expression."

Miss Pollworth raised an eyebrow and replied: "I was merely repeating what my brother said, Margery—"

"Oh, but that is never an excuse for a lady to use improper language! Why, it is slang, I am sure."

"I think you are being very tiresome, my dear. As we are all ladies present, I do not see that it was so very improper. Of course, if there had been a gentleman present, I should not have thought to have said anything of the sort."

Miss Blandish, with a knowing look, smiled and asked: "Would you not if, say, it was Geoffrey here in the room with us?"

"He is my brother—" Pamela began to explain, but Henrietta laughed derisively and declared: "Ah, Geoffrey is not a gentleman, then!"

Before Pamela could think of a retort, Margery, her cheeks now quite scarlet, indignantly stammered: "D-don't you d-dare to imply anything of the sort, Henrietta Blandish. Mr. Pollworth is every inch the gentleman, I'll have you know!"

"Indeed! I never said he was not, my dear. I was only making a bit of fun—But, great heavens, Margery, what is it with you? Have you constituted yourself Geoffrey's champion?"

One would not have thought it possible for Margery's cheeks to achieve a more intense crimson hue, but they did, as she retorted: "I think you are being perfectly odious. Mr. Pollworth is nothing to me, I assure you."

"Henrietta, I pray you will cease to torment Margery," Pamela intervened. "We all know that Margery has a tendre for Geoffrey, and—"

"Oh, Pamela!" wailed Margery. "And I thought you were my friend!"

There was a sparkle of laughter in Pamela's eyes as she turned to Margery and said consolingly: "My dear, there is nothing to be ashamed of. If you like a gentleman, it is far better to admit the fact. In that way no one can have a thing to say to it."

"Oh, but that is not at all the proper thing!" Margery pointed out. "See what Henrietta is trying to make of it."

"Only because you are trying to hide the fact. What is there to hide?"

Margery nodded her head sagely and replied: "Wait 'til you are in love, then you will see how it is. It is quite easy to make little of it, Pamela, when your affections are not engaged—"

"Really, my dears, this conversation has become quite dull," declared Eleanor, shifting her chair back from the hearth. "I do declare the room has grown hot enough to roast one to a turn."

"Yes, it has," agreed Pamela, moving her chair back and throwing off the shawl from about her shoulders. The other ladies began to follow suit while Pamela rang for someone to come and turn down the grate.

The ladies were still in the process of rearranging themselves for greater comfort when the door behind them opened.

"Gibbs, it is an inferno in here. Please to lower the heat," said Pamela, without looking behind.

"Indeed, Pam. Your least desire is my heart's wish!" was the rejoinder as two young gentlemen came into the room and one of them, with a cheery greeting, turned his attention to the hearth.

Immediately there was an exclamation from the ladies, and a flurry of greetings were conferred upon the Honorable Geoffrey Pollworth, who stood rubbing his hands before the fire, and upon the Honorable Kevin Fairchild, who was executing Pamela's request by fiddling with the grate damper.

"I understood that we were experiencing a thaw in this abysmal weather," said Henrietta, "but from the looks of you gentlemen, I judge that it is as cold as ever."

"Not at all, Miss Blandish," replied Geoffrey, still briskly rubbing his hands together. "I'll warrant you it is not springtime out there, but the thaw has set in and quite brought an end to the Frost Fair, dash it all. It was great fun while it lasted."

"The ice has melted?" inquired Margery.

"Yes, it has, and it was almost as much fun to watch as the Fair itself. You ought to have seen it, my dear. All those people scrambling about, trying every which way to save their pots and pans and what have you. A number of them tumbled into the Thames, I'll have you know."

"Oh, those poor unfortunate people!" she cried.

"Bah! They got a bit of a freeze, I should surmise, but what is that to the loss of the Fair? It was such fun—and, in any case, I assure you that a lot of them garnered a pretty penny they never would have seen, otherwise."

At this point, Kevin stood up from the grate and exclaimed: "There! I think that will do it!" He turned about and looked at Pamela.

"Are you a bit more comfortable, Pam?" he inquired, his tone colored with a warmth that was more than friendly.

"Thank you, Kevin. It was most kind of you," she replied. "There is some hot coffee. May I pour you a cup?"

"Please."

Geoffrey laughed. "All the advantage of being a brother! I say, Sis, am I an orphan?"

"Kevin is a guest. You can pour your own."

"Oh, Mr. Pollworth, I should be more than pleased to pour you a cup of coffee—i-if you wish," offered Margery.

Geoffrey bowed gallantly to her, and with a charming smile, replied: "Thank you, Miss Dawley, that is most kind of you."

While the two girls took their turn at the little urn,

Geoffrey turned to his sister and inquired: "I say, Pam, has his lordship been asking after me?"

"No, not that I have heard. Are you expecting something from his quarter? I pray you are not in any trouble."

"Really, Pam, we have company present! Of course, I am not in any trouble. I have merely requested my lord for permission to set up in my own lodgings, and he is giving the matter due consideration."

The tone of Pamela's laughter was somewhat derisive. "Indeed! Your own quarters! Really, Geoffrey, what need have *you* to live away from home? It is not as if you had some business, leagues away. It is only in London you would be staying, and as this is the best of neighborhoods, I do not see what you would have to gain by it."

Geoffrey conferred a look of disdain upon his sister. "You would never understand."

Said Kevin: "I fear you do not understand the way of things, Pam. As a matter of fact, I shall be setting up in my own lodgings, once this beastly weather departs. My father promised it me on condition that I finish my studies. Now, it seems to me, as Geoffrey has come along with me, to the end of our days at Oxford, he ought to have his own quarters, too."

"Really, Kevin," replied Pam, "that is a matter for Lord Pollworth to decide, don't you think?"

"Oh, of course!" Kevin agreed fulsomely. "It was just that I was attempting to show that it was not an unheard-of practice."

Rejoined Pamela, ungraciously: "I thank you for the counsel, Mr. Fairchild."

As Kevin's smile waned, Margery declared: "But, Pamela, it is the most natural thing in the world!

12

Once a creature has grown, it must leave its nest. Just look at birds!"

"Miss Dawley, my brother Geoffrey is neither a bird nor a creature, in the event that you have not noticed. Nor do I see the necessity for his abandoning his home just because he has finished his schooling. I passed beyond lessons ages ago, yet no one has raised the least fuss about my continuing on in this, my home."

"Oh, but that is different! You are a female! You had no need to go to the University. Heavens, how could a female child of thirteen, or so, be expected to live away from home!"

There was a sparkle in Pamela's eye as she replied; "At thirteen, I was a deal more up to snuff than Geoffrey is at eighteen."

Geoffrey let out a guffaw. "There's a loving sister for you! To hear her tell it, she is the older of us by a year, when it is quite the other way about."

"Geoffrey, were you a true gentleman, you would never refer to a lady's age!" Pamela snapped.

Eleanor broke in at this point. "Pamela, why do you not spare us these little contentions between you and Geoffrey. Goodness knows, but I have enough of them at home, with Kevin."

Henrietta tried to second her suggestion by remarking: "I wish I had a brother. You would, too, if you had none."

Geoffrey grinned at her. Then he bowed. "My dear Miss Blandish, I would gladly make the exchange if it were at all possible."

"And I, Henrietta, would not raise the least objection," added Pamela.

"Enough! Enough!" cried Kevin. "If I were you, old man, I should think to look in upon my father to hear his decision—"

"No!" exclaimed Pamela. "Not until you have told us all about the Frost Fair. It has been most unfair for us to have been kept from it, because of the cold and the danger, when actually, thousands upon thousands have visited it without harm. Kevin, what was it like?"

"Yes, Kevin, do tell us. Was it truly a fair like the country fairs? I mean to say, there has never been any such thing in London for as long as I can remember. After all, London is a city, so that any such entertainment would have to be a city fair—not that I have the vaguest idea of what a city fair would be like."

"Oh, Henrietta, must you always play the fool?" commented Pamela. "A fair is a fair!"

"Then pray tell me, if you are so knowledgeable, what is any fair like? I admit I have never been to a one of them," said Henrietta with a half smile.

Pamela chuckled: "No, nor I! So, gentlemen, before you do another thing, you must sit down and inform us of fairs in general, and of the Frost Fair, in particular."

Geoffrey and Kevin exchanged looks. Said Geoffrey: "You are the expert, old chap. Tell 'em!"

Retorted Kevin: "I hardly think so. Came St. Giles Day and you were nowhere to be seen in the precincts of the University—"

"And I dare say no one else was attending classes either—no, not even the professors—"

"It was hardly likely that they should. If you will recall, one of the Doctors of Divinity had the task of carrying out the duties of Clerk of the Market—"

"I say, but that was a sight to see! There he was, dressed to the nines in all scarlet robes, looking a veritable medieval don, inspecting the weighing of cheeses and cuts of beef. I should like to see that done in any *London* market!"

"Aye! In Billingsgate with the fish!"

"Even better, with the fishwives!" chortled Geoffrey in high glee.

"Is that what a fair is like?" inquired Pamela.

"I should hardly think so! It is only because it is held in Oxford that you have all the academic trimmings. I venture to say any fair that is mounted in Cambridge would suffer a similar adornment."

"Geoffrey, you promised to tell us about the Frost Fair. You have yet to begin," Pamela commented.

"Now that is a special sort of celebration. It is a rare thing for the Thames to be frozen over completely, and sufficiently solid to support the weight of a crowd of people. For all we know, it might not happen again in our lifetime."

"I am sure we know all that! Heavens, it has been all the talk for a week! What is going on down at the Thames? What is so disreputable that respectable females are not permitted to enjoy it along with others?" asked Pamela in an urgent tone.

Geoffrey paused and looked at Kevin. "I say, this is getting a bit thick, isn't it?"

Kevin, an expression of uncertainty on his face, shook his head. He turned to the ladies and said, very soberly: "I regret to say that it would not be at all fitting. I mean to say it is something like any other country fair, only more so. The deportment of some of the tradespeople and er—certain representatives of the weaker sex is too shocking by far."

Pamela sat back in her chair, her lips tight with disappointment.

Henrietta remarked: "Gentlemen, you are behaving like a pair of schoolgirls. I mean to say there is no reason for you not to relate to us what is going on upon the ice. I am sure that as you are both bachelors of arts, you have sufficient command of the language to be able to relate the details in less than an offensive manner—or is it that you have managed to come through Oxford as silly as you went in?"

"Do you know that you have a remarkably sharp tongue, Henrietta?" retorted Geoffrey.

"Astonishing, isn't it? And I have not had the benefit of a University schooling. Now, why do you not, the both of you, tell us in simple words all that has gone forward upon the ice of the Thames?"

Kevin was grinning, whereas Geoffrey was pouting. Kevin began: "Actually, from what I have been told, this is not the first time in the annals of London that the Thames has so frozen over. Over a hundred years ago, 1688 in fact, shops were built upon the ice and hackney coaches plied the width of the river as though it were just another London street. And so it has been for the past few days. I dare say, had it not been for the thaw that has commenced, we might have seen the same again. In any case, they got as far as erecting booths of all kinds, conducting business as devoted to eating, drinking, and other diversions. I can assure you that the crowds, who have ventured forth upon the ice, came with empty stomachs and wallets heavy enough to provide a great custom to the venders.

"Within the booths, I do assure you it was as warm as you could wish, for right there upon the ice, fires were built for roasting and mulling and, incidentally, for providing a refuge from the cold without. It warms me much to think on it."

He turned to Geoffrey. "I say, Geoff, do you recall that wag who had one of those booths? He had a sign on it, something to the effect that 'several feet adjoining his premises were to be let on a building lease.' "

"Not really!" exclaimed Geoffrey with a laugh. "I must have missed that one. It was a jolly show, and it would not have hurt if the thaw could have come a week later. Just think of all that would then have occurred. They had got the ice laid out in lanes with ashes strewn along them to give one sure footing—and it was a curious thing, but you never noticed the cold. It was rather exciting to walk about where it had been rushing water but a few days ago."

"And that is what it must be now, once again, blast!"

Said Pamela: "Precisely what is shocking in any of that?"

Geoffrey raised a superior eyebrow. "Nothing at all, I should hope. We are relating only what is fitting and proper for your delicate ears, ladies."

"Oh, fiddlesticks!" commented Pamela.

Henrietta cried: "Do hush, and get on with it! Surely there is something more to make it anything memorable."

"Aye, there is," responded Kevin. "For example, there were swings for the children and there were skittles and knock-'em-downs—anything you might expect at a fair. And, for a fact, an ordinary snuffbox, worth not more than a shilling, was stencilled with the words 'Bought on the Thames,' and those ice-pirates were vending it for three shillings—and so it was with everything that was being sold there, not excluding the food."

"The food, especially," Geoffrey broke in. "To give you some idea of it, there was a business of roasting a sheep over a coal-fire placed in a great iron pan. Just to be a *spectator* at this particular ceremony was a privilege worth sixpence—"

"Aye, Lapland Mutton it was called when it was

17

done," eagerly offered Kevin, "and at a shilling a slice, it did not lack for purchasers!"

"What do you think of that!" exclaimed Geoffrey, grinning. "One-and-six for a slice, because you could not get near to it until you had shelled out the sixpence, you see. And not a bit of bread to go with it. Of course you had to eat it on the spot, or what would have been the fun of it? Just think! Eating a slice of mutton in the midst of the Thames. I shall have something to boast on to my grandchildren, I wager."

"At a shilling and six for a slice of mutton, Brother dear, you'll not have a farthing left over to feed your children, much less your grandchildren. I venture to say that if Papa ever heard of such nonsense, there would be no separate lodgings for you. You did buy yourself a slice, did you not?"

Kevin immediately picked up the narrative. "And then there were quite a number of printers who set up their presses on the ice. They, too, were shovelling money into their pockets in exchange for bits of doggerel, printed up for the occasion, commemorative of the 'Great Frost.' One of them had the wit to sign all his pieces, 'From the presses of Father Thames'!"

"And, of course, you would never have left the ice but you had purchased a sheet," said Eleanor.

Kevin laughed. "As a matter of fact, I have got it with me now. As I do not care for mutton, I thought it would be something, even more substantial, to show to my future offspring."

The ladies implored him to show it to them and he brought it forth from a breast pocket.

It was a broadside of a crude woodcut, showing people and booths, upon a blank plain. There were a few small vessels sprouting out of the featureless

18

ground to suggest the incongruity of the location, and
below the picture was the following verse:

"You that walk here, and do design to tell
Your children's children what this year befell
Come, buy this print, and it will then be seen
That such a year as this hath seldom been."

There was much chattering and passing of the broadside back and forth, as the ladies satisfied their curiosity. Finally, Pamela spoke up.

"It looks like great fun. I wish I could have visited
it. Was that all that was available?"

Again Geoffrey looked uncomfortable. "It was like
any other fair, except that it was held out upon the
Thames. There were some doings that were not at all
nice. Naturally, there were makeshift taverns. The
least pretentious of them had the most impressive
sign: The Crown, and it had a very sad version of that
headgear done up in yellow paint for gilt—"

"But what was there to eat? In the midst of winter,
and a very cold one at that, I should hardly imagine
there could have been nothing but the mutton."

"At the prices they were charging, never fear. You
could have had your choice of savory pies, sausages,
gingerbread, nuts—that sort of thing—"

"It sounds perfectly loathsome! I am happy that I
did not go!"

"Then you are in a very small minority, Sis, for you
could not count the numbers of people who came out
to the Fair every day."

"What has that to say to anything? I have a very
good idea that the people who congregated upon the
Thames were something less than competent to judge
cuisine."

"Cuisine?" expostulated Geoffrey, with a laugh. "Cuisine à la Thames! I say, Kevin, what a shame! We

19

could have made a fortune if we had thought to set up a booth. I can see the sign! Cuisine à la Thames—Chief Cook, the Honorable Geoffrey Pollworth—or would you rather have the honor, old boy?"

"How very funny you have become on a sudden, Brother dear! In the midst of your foolery, I still must point out to you that if you are speaking of cuisine then it is a chef, and not a chief cook, you will require."

Geoffrey brought his hand up to his forehead in an overly dramatic manner and reached a hand to Kevin's shoulder. "My friend, it has begun again! We are about to receive a dissertation on the advantages of the culinary arts of the Frogs. I, being a true and blue Englishman with a love for the native dishes of my homeland, am staggered beyond endurance. My heart fails me! My limbs tremble and I quake all over! Pray, have pity on me! Give me your hand, O! trusty chum, and lead me from this unnatural sister with whom I have been blessed!"

"You are an idiot, Geoff—but, as I have other business, and so do you, let us say good-bye to the ladies."

He grabbed Geoffrey by the hand and towed him out of the room, grinning and waving as he went.

Chapter II

"Brothers!" exclaimed Pamela, even before the two gentlemen were out of earshot. "One would think that the cuisine anglais could not be improved upon."

As the door closed behind them, Eleanor inquired: "Has not Lord Pollworth engaged a chef yet, Pam?"

There was a distressed air about Pamela as she shook her head. "It is beyond belief, and I know it, but my lord has not engaged a chef. We have still to suffer under the odious cookery of a Mrs. Biggam. Here we have just settled ourselves in this new part of town and, still, we cannot boast a fine table. I have made all manner of representations to my lord and my lady, but they will not listen."

"Oh, but my dear, how do they expect to entertain?" Eleanor inquired in a commiserating tone. "I mean to say it has been the thing for ages now to have a chef in one's kitchen. Why, yours must be the only household in Mecklenburg Square not to have a Frenchman in the scullery!"

"Ah yes, it is too true," said Pamela in a mournful tone. "But there is not a thing I can say to it. Papa went to great trouble to secure the services of Mrs. Biggam, and he cannot be persuaded to part with her."

"Pray, what is so special about Mrs. Biggam?"

"Mrs. Biggam prepares all the dishes that my lord was used to as a child," she said dryly.

"Pamela, you have all my sympathy. Whatever shall you do once the weather improves and the season for entertaining begins?"

Pamela bit her lip in consternation and shook her head. "I have thought about it, and I cannot think of a thing. I am sure we shall be dreadfully embarrassed for the poor fare we shall have to offer. Oh dear, I must do something!"

"Oh, I am sure it cannot be all that much of a difficulty," said Henrietta. "You could engage one yourself. Once he is ensconced in the kitchen, and his lordship tastes the delicacies he will prepare, he cannot help but approve."

"But what if he does not? In any case, who am I to go and seek out a French chef? I should not know how to begin."

Henrietta replied: "I should imagine that one goes to a labor exchange and puts in one's order. Have your butler do it. I am sure that he must know how the business is done."

"Gibbs? I think not. He knows his lordship's views on the matter and would never dare to go against his master. In fact, I have not a doubt but that Gibbs would go immediately to his lordship and reveal anything that I had told him."

"Besides," broke in Margery, "It is not only Lord Pollworth that is concerned, but Mr. Pollworth, too. I should never think it fitting to go against the expressed wishes of the men of the family. They always know what is best."

The three other ladies turned to stare at her. Finally, Eleanor shook her head sadly and said: "Dear Margery, you have so much to learn. It *is* a shame that you have no brother in your family. Rely upon it, my dear, the men of the family know next to nothing of what is best for them. Now, in this day and age, it is essential for a proper entertainment that French cuisine be set before your guests. If you do not have a chef then you must engage one, if only for the purpose of the party you are planning."

"But I am not planning any party," responded Margery, puzzled.

"In that case, you will not need the services of a French chef," rejoined Eleanor with a laugh.

Margery laughed too, and added: "It is all right. We have a chef in our kitchen, so I guess I shall not have to worry."

Eleanor had a quizzical look for a moment, but she shrugged it away and addressed her next remark to Pamela.

"Pam, I think you had better converse with your mother on the subject and let her speak to the point with your father. Perhaps, it is because you have not been in Mecklenburg Square for very long that she has not come to realize anything less than a French table will be poorly regarded. I take it that your family is not of London originally?"

"Oh, we have been to London before this. We came up from the family seat in Surrey, for the reason that Geoffrey has come down and Papa wishes to see him

23

established in a good post. If he can find some nobleman active in politics and in need of a secretary, he thinks it will be excellent experience for Geoffrey. Then Geoffrey can assist him with his business, you see, after a time."

"And, of course, there is the business of introducing *you* into Society, too," suggested Henrietta.

"Yes, there is that too—but I do not think I shall make a splash with only Mrs. Biggam to cook for us."

Eleanor, a wise look on her face, said: "You shall have to speak with Lady Pollworth, Pam. You can tell her that all of her neighbors have a Frenchman in their employ. She cannot help but understand the necessity, then."

"I shall certainly make the attempt. You can see how desperate I have become."

"By the way, I understand that the Duke of Pevensey has had a falling out with his man. Perhaps, you and Lady Pollworth could send for the fellow. He just might be happier to be working for someone else at this juncture," suggested Henrietta.

"Is he French?" inquired Pamela.

"Do you think for one minute that a duke would have anything but a Frenchman to cook for him?"

"True. Er—would you know how one goes about sending for the fellow?"

"I should imagine a simple note would be all that was required. If he came, then you would have your chance at him. If he did not, you would have lost nothing, and could proceed to look in another quarter, the labor exchange, for an instance."

"Hmmm. I think that is a very fine idea. Thank you, Henrietta."

At that moment, the butler entered to inform the

young ladies that their carriages had arrived and were waiting their pleasure to carry them home.

"Oh, I detest the thought of having to go out in the cold!" exclaimed Henrietta, rising.

Eleanor and Margery arose, too, and Pamela accompanied them out, expressing her thanks for their having called upon her. At that point, Lady Pollworth made her appearance. There were introductions all round, followed immediately by farewells.

Eleanor waited until Henrietta and Margery had left before she turned to Lady Pollworth and remarked: "Lady Pollworth, may I have your permission to entertain Pamela with un petit dejeuner in the not too distant future?"

As she made the request, she winked at Pamela.

Lady Pollworth blinked in surprise, then she smiled and replied: "How very sweet, my dear. I am sure Pamela will be delighted to accept your invitation. Good-bye, dear, and do carry my best regards to Lady Fairchild. Please to let her know that I have received her card and am planning a small dinner party to which I pray it will be her pleasure to attend. I shall send a note with the particulars very soon."

Eleanor assured her that she would so inform her mother and departed.

"A charming girl, Miss Fairchild," murmured Lady Pollworth.

"Yes, I am so pleased that we moved to Mecklenburg Square. All the young ladies you saw are ever so nice. I am sure that we shall be able to spend pleasant times together."

"Yes, my dear," replied Lady Pollworth absently, as they repaired to the sitting room the company had just vacated. "It is always like this when one moves into a new neighborhood, except that in the city it is quite different."

Mother and daughter sat down together as her ladyship went on.

"There is just so much to do, so many neighbors one must pay one's respects to. It is *never* so much trouble in the country. There the distances may be greater; but, still, there are never so many people!"

"But that makes it so much more fun, Mama! See, but this morning, how many friends I have had to call upon me. In the country, for one reason or another, it would have been weeks before I should have had such an opportunity to entertain."

"Precisely. Everything goes at a great pace in the city. I could wish I had time to think, to prepare, child. I tell you it overwhelms a body."

"I am sure we shall grow accustomed to it. Perhaps, this odious weather will prove a godsend, Mama. It allows us a chance to settle ourselves and make proper preparation to entertain our neighbors and friends in a manner fitting to our station."

"Fitting to our station? What a curious remark, Pamela. I am quite sure that the Pollworths have not a thing to be ashamed of—"

"Of course, we do not, Mama. Nor was I implying that we ever failed to make a proper showing. It is just that in the city, things are different, and what might do quite well in the country—well, I do not think that one can offer the sort of refreshments that are unexpectional in Surrey and think that they will do quite well here in London."

"What in the world are you talking about, child?" said Lady Pollworth. "I do declare I do not understand your nonsense."

"I am trying to tell you that we have got to make a

better arrangement in our kitchen if we are going to maintain the good opinion of our callers."

"Our kitchen? I do not think there is anything wrong in our kitchen, or Mrs. Biggam would have informed me."

"It is Mrs. Biggam who is the trouble. She cannot do the cuisine française."

Lady Pollworth laughed. "Of course, she cannot! Why should she? We are all of us English under this roof, I should like to think. French cookery, indeed! Pamela, I pray you are not about to trouble me again with this wish of yours for a Frenchman in our kitchen. The very idea of a man belowstairs is enough to give one the shudders."

"Oh, Mama, how you talk! Have we not Gibbs and the footmen belowstairs at this very moment?"

"I should hope not. We are not paying them to be belowstairs when their duties require them to be at their posts," said Lady Pollworth, smiling at her own wit.

"I pray you will be serious for a moment. I assure you it is a most important matter. Everyone, who is anyone, has a chef here in the city. It is expected, I tell you. I have just been discussing the matter with my friends. All of them, without exception, have chefs, and they are not about to be impressed with us if we do not."

Lady Pollworth's smile faded. "Are you sure of this, Pamela?"

"But, of course, I am sure. It is what I have been trying to tell Papa and you ever since we came to the city. Mrs. Biggam is quite unexceptional in Surrey; but, here, in the city, in the house of Lord Pollworth, she has no place."

"Oh dear! Just see what comes of not having sufficient time to call upon my neighbors. I must wait for my daughter to inform me of domestic matters. I told your father that we were rushing the business, but he would never listen. Now see what comes of it! Why, we could be deeply embarrassed! Not only in this, but in heaven knows what other matters as well!"

"Mama, that is all well and good and I am sure you are right, but we have this business of our cuisine right in front of our eyes, and, it seems to me, we ought to remedy the situation at once. We must take one embarrassment at a time as we come to it."

"But, child, you do not know the half of it. One does not give the sack to a good woman like Mrs. Biggam, and one does not go out, on an instant's notice, and engage a French cook. I should not know where to begin."

"I have heard that there might be an excellent fellow looking to change masters—"

"Masters! Yes, that is the trouble! It is your father. He will never sit still for it, I tell you. You know what my lord is like. He is John Bull himself when it comes to anything foreign—and, I cannot say that I blame him, you know. I mean to say we *are* English."

"It seems to me that what is good enough for a duke ought to be unexceptional to us—and I mean an *English* duke!"

Lady Pollworth regarded her daughter blankly.

"Mama, it certainly is not an exceptional thing to follow the trend of fashion, and having a chef in a noble household, has been quite the fashion for many years—"

"It was all due to that horrid affair! I was a girl when it all took place—twenty-five years ago—Heavens! Can it have been as long ago as that—?"

It was now Pamela's turn to look blank.

28

"Mama, what in the world are you talking about? We were discussing the procurement of a chef—"

"I beg your pardon, dear, but I was thinking of all the French people who came to our shores because of their horrid revolution. That is when it started you know—this cuisine of theirs."

Pamela chuckled. "I do believe you are confused. I am sure the French have been at cooking for at least as long as the English have."

"But of course they have! It was their revolution, I am sure, that sent them scurrying to England for their lives, and naturally they brought their cooking with them," retorted her ladyship. "I am sure if there had not been so many of them, we should not have had this inundation of French cooks and French valets and French footmen—" She stopped abruptly and frowned.

"A duke?" she asked. "What about a duke?"

Pamela frowned for a second, until she could catch on to the thread of her mother's thinking, smiled, and replied: "It was the Duke of Pevensey I had reference to. Eleanor Fairchild believes that his chef is dissatisfied with his post and would be available—"

"Ah yes, the Fairchild girl. Isn't she lovely? She has such a fine manner about her—and there is excellent family. Has your brother met her?"

"Why yes, Geoffrey has met all my new friends. He and Kevin—that is Eleanor's brother—joined us for a moment, but it was not the first time—"

"Oh dear, I wish I were as young as you, my sweet. It is so much easier when you are young. One does not have to stand upon such ceremony, you see—"

"Mama, about the Duke of Pevensey's chef!"

Lady Pollworth frowned. "Who is the Duke of Pevensey? The title is not familiar to me."

"I do not know, but I can look him up in Debrett's."

"If we are about to inherit his Grace's cook, I should think it is the least we can do," replied her ladyship.

Pamela arose and went over to a small table just off the hearth. Reposing on it was a bulky tome which she picked up and brought back to her chair. She sat down and began to go through the book.

"He is older than Papa. He was born in '58—"

"How old is the duchess, dear?"

"Her birth is given as '56—"

"Then she is a good deal older than I," remarked her ladyship, a contented look spreading over her countenance. "And their children? Is there an heir?"

"Yes. There are a son and two daughters, the son being the eldest."

"How interesting. The son, how old is he?"

"His name is Gerald John Frederick and he was born in 1786. He is twenty-eight years old, which makes him eleven years older than I. I fear he is much too old for me to hope to become a duchess through his offices," she said with a little laugh.

"Rubbish! I am sure that is a fine age for your husband, my dear. At his age, he cannot be counted a child any longer and has come to a proper station in life. I see nothing wrong with the idea."

"Mama, we are only planning to win his cook. Besides, as the daughter of a baron, I can have little charm for so high a personage as a marquess."

"His father has settled a title on him? How very nice. I should think it would be rather thrilling to marry a marquess, and when his Grace went to join his ancestors, my daughter would be elevated to the rank of duchess."

Pamela laughed. "Indeed, it would be very nice. We

must have his Grace and the marquess over for dinner some night," she said, lightheartedly.

"Do you truly believe they would come, dear?"

This time Pamela's laughter was gleeful. "Oh, Mama, how can you think it! Of course, they would not accept. Who are we to take the notice of the Duke of Pevensey?"

Lady Pollworth was quite serious as she proceeded to point out that, as they would be hiring the duke's chef, he was bound to notice.

"I hardly think that engaging his chef will qualify us for his acceptance. You would not think anything of some cit who had taken a fancy to Mrs. Biggam—not for that reason, at any rate."

"If the fellow was not in our circle, I certainly would not, but I should be highly wroth with anyone who steals my servants from me. Only when I have become dissatisfied with their service and have discharged them would I tolerate such attentions. It is unthinkable that I should deign to notice such a person—except in the matter of references, of course."

"That is precisely how his Grace would feel about our engaging his chef—"

"Oh, Pamela, I should hate to cause the gentleman any offense! He would never notice us then and would have every right to cut us."

"But, as he is not satisfied with his chef, it will not happen that way, Mama."

"Then, there is nothing to worry about. I shall send a polite note to the duke—"

"No, no, it is not necessary. We are not dealing with his Grace; we are treating with his chef. I am sure that we do not have to bother the duke even for references. The chef must be all that one could wish."

Lady Pollworth frowned. "Not to ask his Grace for a

reference would be most exceptional, my dear. He would think that we were ignoring him."

Pamela sighed. "Oh, very well, we shall request a reference from his Grace if it is so important."

"It is. If his Grace is dissatisfied with the fellow, we have a right to know what was the cause of the difficulty between them. Heavens, if it should prove the Frenchman is forever in his cups, I would have his Grace know that we, at Pollworth House, are not about to put up with anything so disgraceful, either."

"I suppose you are right. Perhaps I had better speak with Eleanor about this fellow and learn all I can. It is just that it would be so perfect if we could boast that we have got Pevensey's chef in our kitchen."

"Yes, dear, you go and do just that whilst I have a word with your father on this score. Of course, we cannot proceed with this without his approval."

"Oh, but, Mama, it is hopeless then!" protested Pamela. "Papa has made his feelings known on the subject more than once, and at no time has he looked with approval. Why, as far as he is concerned, Mrs. Biggam is one of the family!"

"Now, now, Pamela, do not speak disrespectfully of your father. He is the master in this house and, under this roof, his word is law. Never you mind, but leave your father to me. I shall bring him 'round. If a Frenchman is necessary in one's kitchen, then the Pollworths will have a Frenchman in their kitchen!"

Chapter III

As Lord Pollworth and his son came to join the ladies before going into dinner, one might have been excused for taking the baron for a dandy. It was true that he was dressed in the latest style and that style had been set, in every detail, by the Regent's favorite, George Brummel. Beau Brummel, as he had come to be known, not being a man for active pursuits, yet desirous of being comfortable in his attire, had adopted a costume that was neither extreme in its snugness of fit, nor in its distortion of a gentleman's figure. It struck a happy medium amongst the fashions that had been modish in recent years, so that many gentlemen, Lord Pollworth amongst them, were pleased to adopt the new apparel, knowing that they were in fashion without having recourse to corsets and other painful appurtenances; that is, gentlemen like Lord Pollworth who were not burdened with too much flesh.

33

Geoffrey, this evening, was obviously on his best behavior, and the reason was quickly known. His lordship had promised to converse with him, after dinner, over their port, until the ladies came to join them. The topic was to be Lord Pollworth's decision with respect to his wish for an establishment of his own.

As the family proceeded into the dining room, Pamela suffered a qualm. She had not been able to learn from her mother when her ladyship would confront his lordship with the Pollworth's need for a revised cuisine. She knew her mother well enough to fear that it could happen at any time, and so she prayed that her father would be in an expansive mood. Otherwise, a tempest might ensue over the dinner table, leading to all manner of unpleasantness. It had happened before, in her own case, and she was not sure that his lordship was at all prepared to entertain the suggestion so soon again.

She would have preferred to let matters stand until she was able to verify the facts regarding the Pevensey chef. At the moment she could not even supply his name, and she doubted very much if her father had any knowledge of his Grace. Since her mother was not given to explanation, Pamala hoped that she herself would be present to supply whatever information her father might require for his deliberations on the matter.

The dinner proved as English as English could be. Mrs. Biggam had prepared, and Gibbs proceeded to serve with the assistance of the two footmen, old-fashioned slit leek soup, removed with a second course consisting of a boiled chicken at top, a fine haunch of venison at bottom—it was not the haunch's first appearance at table—ham on one side, a flour pudding on the other, and beans in the middle.

Pamela's spirits rose, even if her stomach gurgled a bit in protest at the encore appearance of the venison. It was just possible that her father would be disappointed with Mrs. Biggam's efforts this evening.

But, no, Lord Pollworth, after the soup, regarded the main course with great approval and exclaimed: "Ah, what a prize we have in our good Mrs. Biggam. Look you, everyone, at this fine English cookery! It is hearty and it is wholesome, and what is more, when one tucks into it, one knows precisely what one is dining upon.

"I have, in my frequent visits to certain clubs about Town, been prevailed upon to sample dishes that bear no resemblance to the delicious viands from which they have been prepared. So altered are they by spices and spirits that one is hard put to determine if it is a savory or a proper dish. It is this infernal French cookery—ha! they would have it, cuisine! I do not fault them. Cuisine it must be, for it is never cookery in any language, I tell you. I do not know what we should have done for sustenance if we had not thought to bring Mrs. Biggam up from Surrey with us.

"Everything, here in London, is drowned, I tell you, positively drowned in these fluid, ill-tasting disguises that are called sauces. Sauces, bah! Sauces, humbug! They are not sauces at all but concoctions for depraved palates! Aye, it is a conspiracy I tell you. The French are at perverting our hearty English dishes to effeminate pap. I should not be in the least surprised if this is not some trick of that wily Bonaparte to conquer Britain with dishes that are fit for only a—a Frenchman!"

"My lord, you are waxing choleric. It will do little to settle these dishes, you are so enamored of, and you will suffer grave distress. I pray you postpone this discourse until we have finished dining," Lady Pollworth suggested mildly.

Lord Pollworth accepted the admonishment and the meal progressed without further interruption. Pamela's appetite was not helped by this outpouring of her father's views and she was glad when the cover was removed and a syllabub and gooseberries were served for the dessert.

Soon thereafter, Lady Pollworth and Pamela left the gentlemen to their port, white and red, and retired to the drawing room.

"It does not look well, Mama. You heard Papa going on about cookery and cuisine. He is not about to allow us a French cook."

Lady Pollworth did not appear to be very encouraging as she remarked: "No, I presume that our lord and master will prove rather intransigent in the matter, but he will have to be brought round. Perhaps, my pet, after he has had a chance to witness how things are done in the fashionable households that we shall be visiting in the next few weeks, he will suffer a change of heart. No, I do not think it wise to broach the problem to him at this particular moment."

"But, then, we shall have lost our chance to procure the Pevensey chef! It is such a good chance, Mama, that the thought of missing it makes me quite ill."

"Fiddlesticks, child! The Pevensey Frenchman is not the last Frenchman in the world. I am sure that there are plenty of others who would be only too happy to serve in such a respectable domicile as is ours. You know, my dear, the Pollworths are not a lowly people.

Your father had not the least trouble in gaining access to his clubs. He had his choice of quite a few before he settled on White's. It is a gentleman's club out of the top drawer; a most conservative institution, I understand. So you see, my child, even his choice of clubs is influenced by his opinion of what constitutes good cookery."

"Papa chose White's for its table?"

Lady Pollworth nodded and smiled. "Indeed he did. It is a proper club where an English gentleman is sure to find his beefsteak and boiled fowl, with an apple tart for dessert. Those were his very words."

"How very odd," said Pamela, faintly.

Her brother's beaming face, as the gentlemen, having finished their drink, came into the drawing room to be with the ladies for a short time before retiring, did not penetrate to Pamela's thinking. She was completely absorbed in her own thoughts.

"I say!" exclaimed Geoffrey, his face aglow with satisfaction. "I say, hear the wonderful news! Papa has given his permission for me to move out to my own quarters, and I am to have a hundred pounds the quarter for pocket money whilst he foots my bills!"

Lady Pollworth smiled at him and said: "I pray that you will not spend it foolishly, my son, and have a care with what companions you associate yourself."

"I shall join Kevin Fairchild at his lodgings. We have got it all planned. I tell you it will be smashing!"

"Of course, my lady, as I have explained it to Geoffrey, it will not be all play for him. I shall be on the lookout for a post to suit his qualifications for bachelor of arts, and he will be expected to apply himself so that I may have me a trusted assistant in later years," stated Lord Pollworth. "As a matter of fact, I am quite proud of my son. There was a time when I would never have admitted as much; the time when we were all quite certain he should be sent down. But, I was so relieved when the business was got over and he went on to finish his courses. There are not many gentlemen in my acquaintance who can boast a bachelor of arts in the family—and they all of them have sons who attended University too.

"This Fairchild lad must be quite an adornment to his father, too, I ween."

"Yes, my lord, I should think so," agreed her ladyship. "They have got a very handsome daughter into the bargain. I had the pleasure of meeting her today."

Lord Pollworth turned to Pamela. "And how goes it with the daughter of the house, my pet?"

"Quite well, Papa, quite well. Is it true, Papa, that you elected White's to be your club only because of the food that was served there?"

His lordship frowned. "I should say not! Where could you have gained such a silly notion? White's is, above all, a club for Tories. Not all Tories, mind you; but those gentlemen who are the finest gentlemen in the land, and to whom His Majesty must ever turn to in his efforts to maintain the constituted authority and the church of the realm. That is why I elected to become a member of White's. It is obvious that such a body of English gentlemen could be satisfied with nothing less than the best of English cookery in their dining rooms, and so it is with their club."

"If I may be excused," said Pamela, "I shall retire. Congratulations to you, Geoffrey. I wish you joy in your new lodgings. I shall miss not having you about."

There was something so mournful in her tone that Geoffrey quickly assured her he would not be absent from the family table all that much. But, of course, he would miss her, too, and Papa and Mama as well.

Pamela did not go directly to bed. She was not tired and had no need of slumber at that moment. In fact, sleep was the farthest thing from her mind. She was too upset to sleep, and she was too upset to have remained behind to celebrate Geoffrey's good fortune.

There was something akin to jealousy filling her breast at the moment. No, it was not the fact that Geoffrey was about to go out on his own in the world. She was a female, and the security of a home, coupled with the affection of a gentleman who loved her, was all she could aspire to, and all she wished for.

Geoffrey had got his dearest wish fulfilled. That was the thing that was filling her with unhappiness for herself. She was now a Londoner, but not an ordinary Londoner. She was the daughter of a wealthy baron, and as such, it was expected that she would make an excellent marriage. She had been bred to expect it, and as a result, it was *her* dearest wish. But, if she were not to have all the advantages that went with her exalted social position, it was likely that the best of suitors would not find their way to Pollworth House.

Her friends had assured her that a French chef was not all-important to her station, but it was expected in London these days. The thing of it was, that if word got round that the Pollworths had not even a French chef, questions would be asked, and it was certain to be remarked upon in a derogatory fashion.

This was Pamela's thinking today, and she had no doubt but that it was a true reflection of her time and set. It had not always been so.

*　　*　　*

Almost five months ago, Lord Pollworth had announced to his nearest and dearest, under the roof of the family seat near Guildford, Surrey, his considered resolve to move the family to a house in London.

He had declared: "Clandon Park has proved a most commodious and enjoyable residence for the time that we have spent here; but the times have changed, my dears, and so must we. In fact, the children are grown and needs must have the room to spread their wings, as the saying goes, and Guildford is a poor place for them to do so with any effect.

"More than this, the war has been going unsteadily so that business ventures are calling for attention. My own, which have been managed handily by my agents in London, until now, have not called for my attention overmuch. This, too, has changed, and I must now see to them myself, giving the greatest attention to the family's prospects which, of course, are so heavily dependent upon the investments in Consols. It is conceivable that I may have to withdraw some of these funds and find other, more profitable avenues of investment in order to protect the equities. It is all in accordance with the fortunes of war, you will understand.

"In any case, it will provide our son, Geoffrey, his opportunity to become a man of the world. Had this war been over and done with, and the Continent open once again, it would have been my dearest delight to have accompanied him on a grand tour, even as did my father with myself. Under the present circumstances, when he has come down from Oxford, I shall be able to introduce him into the society of business in the capital of world finance, London.

"As for our dear daughter, Pamela, think what an opportunity it can prove! The highest levels of fashionable Society will be opened to her, and one may hope that she will not be long in establishing a prosperous future for herself, one that we can approve and bless with all our hearts."

It was a long speech, and neither Pamela nor Lady Pollworth thought it required such a long-winded declamation. Both ladies were shocked at the suddenness of the news but pleasantly, even if her ladyship was thrown into confusion.

"Frederick, this is so sudden!" she exclaimed. "You never mentioned a word of it to me!"

"Yes, my dear, and I apologize. It is the war, you see. It is possible we have done Bonaparte's business for him, but then again, one—"

"Oh, not that I pray! I am sure I should never understand a word of it. It is enough, dear Husband, that you have spoken your mind to me. I am sure that I shall enjoy a short sojourn in London, and we shall not lose too much of the Season—"

"Madam, what are you saying? We shall be there for the start of the Season, I do assure you."

"Frederick, how can you say such a thing? By the time we have found us a place to stay, and by the time we have put things in readiness to depart, why we shall be fortunate indeed if we can manage any part of the Season."

"My dear Constance, we do not have all the time in the world—and you may expect to be staying on in London for quite a while. I have no idea, at the present moment, how long it will be.

"As for a place to stay, there is a district where many fine homes are a-building, many of them already erected on speculation, and only the finest families welcomed. I have purchased such a house. It is in

41

Bloomsbury, not far from the new museum. All is in readiness to receive us."

Lady Pollworth looked aghast at the news. She raised a hand to clutch her throat and gasped: "But what of Clandon House? Have you sold it?"

Lord Pollworth smiled. "Sell the family seat? Of course, I would not. No, I have arranged to lease it on the understanding that, with the exception of Gibbs and Mrs. Biggam, the present servants may stay on if they choose."

"But Gibbs—and Mrs. Biggam? Oh, you cannot be so heartless as to dismiss them."

"Not at all. They shall come with us. I do not think I should care to have to get used to a London butler, and certainly not for what goes by the name of cook in that city."

Seeing that his lady was at a loss for words, his lordship added some persuasion.

"You will see it shall all work out for the best. It is time that Geoffrey learned the ways of the city and, I do assure you it will enable Pamela to mix in the best circles, something more high-toned than anything Surrey has to offer."

"Yes, yes," murmured her ladyship, absently.

Pamela was thrilled! She could hardly contain herself. Immediately she was at her father with all sorts of questions. This gave Lady Pollworth a chance to recover.

"Just a moment, Pamela. I have a wish to say something to your father," she interrupted. "Frederick, precisely when is it that you have it in mind to remove us to London?"

"As I have said, there is a house, a very fine house, awaiting us in the city, and there is nothing to keep us here. Geoffrey will be down from Oxford, and I hope that we shall be able to receive him there, rather than here. I am sure, with Gibbs to assist you—and Pamela, too—you can be got ready in four or five days—"

"Never, Frederick! Never on my life can we be got ready in so little time! Why, there would be no time at all to take our leave of the neighbors, not even time to have a dinner—or a rout—or—"

"My love, this is serious business. If all of that is so very important to you, very well, I shall go on to London, prepare the house in the best way I see fit, and you and Pamela can come along after you have had your fill of farewells. The thing of it is that, at any moment, the war might come to an end, and I had better be at my agent's right hand to instruct him with regard to the holdings. After, it will be too late. I ought to be there right now!"

"Oh dear, I dare say that, if you are so determined on it, we shall have to go along with you. I should hate to think how you would manage without me, alone in a great house—and Lord almighty! if it should just be you and Geoffrey—well, it does not bear thinking on! Very well, Frederick, Pamela and I shall be ready within the fortnight."

"The se'ennight, my dear, or I leave without you."

"Oh, you are being so villainous! Pamela, what are we to do? I am sure that I can never prepare myself for the journey in such a very short time. There is not time to breathe, much less pack all the things we shall be needing."

Pamela recalled having gone over to her mother at this point, and assuring her that it certainly was possible. And so it had proved.

If Lord Pollworth had thought to infuse in his wife

and daughter a spirit of enthusiastic cooperation, at the outset at least, he was mistaken. The news served more to immobilize their minds and bodies than anything else. And, as the news pervaded the household, the same effect was to be noted throughout. Before ever a finger was lifted amongst the servants, the question of who was going off with the family to London, and who was remaining behind on the estate, had to be debated and settled. These conversations, of course, drew Lady Pollworth and Pamela into their midst.

Lord Pollworth could say what he liked regarding the problem, but when it came to the ladies' body-servants, his words were completely disregarded.

Making up their minds as to which of their maids and how many were to accompany them gave the ladies some respite, during which they were enabled to come to terms, not only with their lord and master's wishes, but with the suddenness with which he had broached the matter to them. It took them both all of a day to make up their minds about their abigails and the maids who would be assisting, and his lordship was reduced to a state of sputtering indignation when he learned, at the next evening's meal, that nothing very constructive had been achieved with regard to the move.

Lady Pollworth assured her husband that upon the following day, she would personally look into things and give instruction to Gibbs as to what had to be done. Gibbs was a very good sort and could be relied upon.

To her dismay, Lord Pollworth pointed out that it would not be possible for him to dispense with Gibbs' services. He was using the fellow to assist him in arranging his own concerns.

This news brought Lady Pollworth to the verge of tears, as she declared that it would be impossible to proceed without Gibbs. The dear fellow knew where everything was.

"Which is precisely why I have need of him," replied Lord Pollworth. "Surely, there is someone else in this vast domicile with sufficient knowledge to take his place with you."

"Mama, I am sure that we can do it all without Gibbs' assistance. One can always seek him out for a word or two, when it is needed."

"Of course, my dear. I should have no objection to that at all," Lord Pollworth declared.

Finally, everyone at Clandon Park was satisfied that they knew what was about to happen and what would be required of them. In fact, the servants seemed to have a much better idea of the business than did their two mistresses. As things began to settle down and the work commenced, Pamela discovered that her enthusiasm for the undertaking had become a real thing, and she went to work with a will, being quite helpful and, after a few days, quite competent to make the little decisions that were required at almost every turn.

Lady Pollworth, too, found the planning of the arrangements most interesting and shouldered a very great burden all by herself. Each morning, she would instruct whatever group of servants she could manage to collect, in their duties for the day, and then go off to make her farewell calls about the neighborhood.

She was away until early noon, returning home just in time for a nuncheon, after which there would be numberless callers come to return her courtesy, and to see how things were going along with the Pollworths.

By the end of the day, Lady Pollworth was delightfully fatigued, and filled with a great sense of satisfaction for all that she had accomplished. The dining room conversations were larded with her self-commendations and bits of unwanted advice to her husband and daughter as to how the business should be carried forward.

Neither his lordship nor Pamela was surprised. In fact, they were quite relieved to have her ladyship in such excellent spirits—and out of their way, as they proceeded with packing up the household effects, in preparation for the move.

It was not until the Pollworth cavalcade was making its slow progress towards the metropolis that Lady Pollworth, with all the farewell ceremonies behind her, thought fit to inquire of his lordship as to their new location. The matter had become of some importance to her because of the many queries from her neighbors on that score. Since Lord Pollworth had always the excuse of being too concerned with his own business, she had not been able to satisfy herself, or her neighbors, as to the particular quality of the neighborhood, or of the new house itself, for that matter. It was a remark by one of her more knowledgeable cronies in Guildford that was troubling her.

For any traveler, not in haste, the way to London from Guildford was a bare, half day's journey. For the Pollworths, however, in deference to her ladyship's aversion to any speed much greater than a walk, it was bound to take the greater part of the day. In order to insure their arrival in Bloomsbury in the daylight hours, the party had begun their journey at a very early hour.

Lady Pollworth was not all that used to having her mode of living disrupted so radically and was, therefore, forced to spend most of the trip recuperating. By the time she felt herself fit to join in the conversation between her spouse and her daughter, the Pollworth carriages and coaches were approaching the Thames, their destination not far off.

"Frederick, you have never said precisely the sort of neighborhood that we are going to reside in. Now, you have mentioned the fact it is in Bloomsbury, and that does not sit at all well with me. Lady Litwell's face fell when I invited her to call when next she found herself in London.

"It set me to thinking. Is there not a foundling's home in Bloomsbury? I should think that such an institution would add nothing to the respectability of the neighborhood—and, furthermore, it is Bloomsbury, not London. Frederick, I am sure that you would have been wiser to have secured a house in the West End of the city. I understand it is all the crack, there."

Lord Pollworth sighed. "Indeed, my lady, Bloomsbury is beyond the limits of the City of London, but that is nothing. One does not take up his residence in the City if he can help it.

"Bloomsbury for residences is quite new, I assure you. Even as we travel to it, there are new homes being erected—and they are of the finest, you may rely upon it. True, there is the foundling home, but there is the British Museum there as well, and more than one fine square adorns the district.

"Any fears that you might have are groundless. Bloomsbury is quite in the fashion and Mecklenburg Square, being the very latest to have been laid out and built round, is at the height. I can tell you it cost me a pretty penny to purchase the place and that, my dear, must speak volumes to you as to its attractiveness. I am sure you will like it immensely."

"But shan't we be leagues from the shops? Frederick, what is the use of residing in London if one cannot take advantage of all the wonderful shops?"

He laughed. "Bloomsbury is not so far as all that from the heart of things. Besides, you have got your carriage, and you shall have your own coachman, whom you can share with Pamela—although I cannot imagine why the one of you would be occupying it without the other—so that all of London will be accessible to you.

"For my own needs, the situation is most excellent. We shall be far enough removed from the turmoil of the City to be able to pursue our lives in the peace we have known at Clandon Park, but I shall, at a moment's notice, be able to descend into the City where, for the future, my attention must be focused."

It sounded most encouraging to Pamela. True there was in her an uneasiness about having to accommodate herself to a new house, a new neighborhood, and, most important, to new neighbors. It was reasonable to expect that there would be a number of them from excellent backgrounds, comporting themselves in highly polished style. This was cause for her uneasiness. All she had for comparison were the manners current in Surrey. She knew her way in that society had been unexceptional, but it was quite likely that what was unexceptional in Surrey could prove exceptional in London, and she hated the thought that she would not be able to fit in, for being so green.

Her mother had been no help to her at all upon that score. Lady Pollworth had assured her that a lady was a lady, no matter where, and that there was not a thing to be concerned about.

Pamela did not think so, and until it could be set-

tled in her mind, her enthusiasm for the move was
tinged with uncertainty.

The period of intense cold that London suffered that
year, late 1813, caused untold difficulties and outright
hardships to many residents of the city, but it served
to permit the Pollworths an informal introduction to
their neighbors in Mecklenburg Square.

None of the families who had preceded them had
been in residence for very long, so that as newcomers
they were, in truth, not so remarkable. Since the
grand habitations that lined two sides of the square,
the remaining sides still to be built upon, were equipped
with the latest in conveniences, the only hardship
they faced was the bitter cold out-of-doors. They had
the latest in coal-burning stoves and grates to keep
them warm within and, in the comings and goings
about the square, ample opportunity was afforded for
everyone to become informally acquainted, especially
amongst the younger set.

Pamela, being of a quality to match her compeers,
had no difficulty in finding acceptance, and when her
handsome brother, Geoffrey, finally did come down
from Oxford, the popularity of the Pollworths was
firmly established.

Lady Pollworth, as was usual with her, was engaged in planning how she would make her appearance in the Society of Mecklenburg, counting not at
all the fact that she was already in the midst of
visiting and receiving, and being thoroughly confused
by all the new faces and new names that had now
become as the bread of life to her. But, until the
Pollworths had held their first affair to celebrate their
coming amongst the inhabitants of Mecklenburg
Square, she went along on the assumption that she

was not actually in anybody's acquaintance as yet.

Since Lord Pollworth was greatly occupied with the progress of the allies against Napoleon, and was spending most of his days at his club in the City, her ladyship had all the time in the world to set her plans for their very first entertainment in the new dwelling. The fierce cold insured that it would be some time before any one was in a mood to leave the family hearth for visits of any sort, with the result that all social exchanges about the Square were conducted upon the most informal basis.

Pamela had found the business of settling into Mecklenburg Square very interesting, and quite exhilarating. There had been not the least difficulty in getting acquainted with the Fairchilds and that had led easily to being introduced to the other ladies of her age in the immediate vicinity.

Nor was the least of it the fact that it had been Kevin Fairchild who had made the opportunity, and that he was a deal more of a polished gentleman than any of the swains of Surrey.

Then, when Geoffrey had arrived and she had introduced her brother to Kevin, both of them had taken to each other on the spot, and it seemed that everything about Mecklenburg Square had grown quite cozy. The onset of the Great Frost had only accelerated the degree of intimacy in the group, and it was not until this very morning, when the matter of entertaining without a French chef in the kitchen was mentioned, that the first doubts had assailed her.

Chapter IV

Speaking between friends, who were on such warm and intimate terms with her, about the inability of her family to set a proper table, had proved embarrassing, but the embarrassment was not so overwhelming as it would have been had her friends been either total strangers or neighbors of note. Considering the fact that it was rumored two earls and a viscount were expected to be taking up residences on the Square, the matter of being able to provide fitting entertainment loomed large in Pamela's thinking.

Her father, on any other count, need give way to no one in the matter of wealth. Being a female, she had no idea of the sum of his holdings but understood, by reason of their style of living, that the Pollworths were of the "best people," a phrase that implied that Society of people possessing great wealth and being blessed with excellent lineages.

Obviously, the easy acceptance the Pollworths encountered was well understood. Pamela had no reason to doubt that she could look where she pleased for notice or for friendship, anywhere in London. But this could be true only for as long as the family met the requirements of the Society in which they planned to move. She understood this point very well, but she could not understand why his lordship was unable to appreciate its importance.

London was not Surrey, and it seemed to her that they had been quite fortunate in making the transition. It would be a matter of the greatest disappointment if, having come so far, they would jeopardize their social standing because of an omission that was so easily supplied: namely, a French chef.

The more she thought about it, the more she became convinced that something had to be done and done quickly. Any day, now, her mother would extricate herself from her state of chronic confusion, the weather would ameliorate, and the Pollworths would begin to entertain. Before that happened, there was no question but that a French chef of some reputation had to be convinced to take up his post in the Pollworths' kitchen. Only then, could she be sure that her family's station and reputation could be preserved.

It was beyond belief at this point that anything in the way of debate could convince her father his palate was not the dictator of what society expected to see served under the Pollworth roof. Mrs. Biggam, in that regard, just would not do.

If only he would have listened, she could have pointed out the situation with the footmen; how it was the accepted thing that required they have three of the fellows cluttering up the house, when it was perfectly obvious that one footman was as much as was truly required. So it was with the kitchen staff. A French chef was not essential to them, but, if they intended to make any sort of a splash, he was at least as important to their standing as were the three footmen.

Such were Pamela's thoughts as she prepared herself for slumber. Everything went to prove how desperate was the situation. It gave to her a sense of satisfaction to have so thoroughly and rationally established the need for the replacement of Mrs. Biggam by a Gallic successor.

Now, with a clear conscience, she could proceed to consider the next step, which step she had been aiming to accomplish however she might have justified it. There was no doubt in her mind that her mother was not up to the business at all. If her ladyship had *first* to confer with his lordship, then the undertaking was doomed from the start. Obviously, it was all up to herself to see to the business. Unfortunately, she was not put to the trouble of discovering a justification for her, the veriest junior member of the family, to do what was, by right, the responsibility of the lord and master, her father.

After giving it long and serious consideration, she could only conclude that it was a deal easier to justify the need of a chef than it was to justify *her* doing anything about it.

The conclusion did not come as a great surprise to Pamela. For one thing, it was the business of the butler to engage servants, and for another, it was the prerogative of the head of the household to establish the number and the quality of the employees to be hired. As but a child of the house, it never had been, nor was it now, in her power to act in the matter. At best, she could make her wishes known to her mother with regard to her own personal maid, for the lady of the household did have a say with her lord, especially on those matters of domestic service that were the peculiar province of females. But, until Pamela had become mistress of her own domicile, she had very little to say, and in the matter of choosing the culinary staff, she had already had her say, and to no effect.

Truly, she had no alternative in the usual course of things and, by rights, must needs let the matter drop. She could do this with a free conscience, any embarrassment arising from the Pollworths not having a chef would have to be borne by his lordship.

However, this did not sit well with her. It would make no difference in the fashionable world, who was at fault. It would be all the members of the Pollworth family who would be made to suffer, she especially. It was all very well that her father had found it necessary, for business reasons, to remove the family to London, but her interest, was bound to be quite different—and his lordship had been aware of this. By coming to take up their residence in the heart of fashionable Society, it stood to reason that every opportunity must be afforded to the daughter of the household to make the best of things.

What better than that she should make her appearance before the world in a faultless and unexceptional manner? Up to this day, she had been sure that she lacked for nothing, and that her entrance into Society would be a brilliant success, something she could look forward to without a tremor. But, alas, Mrs. Biggam did not fit in the picture at all. A French chef was requisite, and the evidence was all about her. Every one of her new friends could boast of her family's having the best of French cuisine. It was such an obvious thing, why, oh why could not her father understand?

Such thinking was bound to have its effect, and Pamela had soon worked herself into a state of agitation, such that native caution and the demands of decent behavior faded. She gave herself over to considering how she might circumvent her father's wishes.

Once upon a time, Pamela had, in a moment of boredom, worked her way through a few pages of one of her brother's schoolbooks. It was entitled, *The Elements of Euclid,* and filled with curious diagrams, having no meaning for her whatsoever. She gathered from the preface that Euclid was a Greek of long ago, who achieved a measure of fame with these little triangles, and that did not impress her in the least. But she did recall, on a few subsequent occasions, some suggestions contained in the little volume for the use of rigorous reasoning in solving problems.

In her estimation, the present impasse called for the most rigorous sort of reasoning, and so she put her mind to work upon the problem with her recollections of old Euclid to guide her.

The proposition to be defined was quite simple. The Pollworths were in dire need of a French chef. The facts, as given, were quite simple, too. The Duke of Pevensey had a chef who was available, and her father was not interested in pursuing the matter. Well, the conclusion was just as simple. *Ergo*—and that word was right in Mr. Euclid's style—if the Pollworths were to acquire a chef, she would have to do something about it.

Pamela sat back, very pleased with herself. She smiled as she realized that Mr. Euclid had come to the very same conclusion she had reached herself. Now, all that was left to do was to commence the business with all confidence.

Of course it would have to be carried out unbeknownst to her father and her mother. Geoffrey, too. He could never be trusted, and would attempt to dissuade her, besides. As for any of her new friends, she thought not. This was not to be some schoolgirl prank, but would require great judgment and circumspection. She had not known Eleanor, and Henrietta, and Margery long enough to know how they might act with her in the matter. No, if it were done at all, it had best be done by herself.

She went on to consider the how of it. She must pay a call upon the Duke of Pevensey's household—she could find his direction easily enough in *Debrett's* —and—?

Now, there was a bit of a poser! Whom was she to ask for? Never his Grace—or the duchess, either. Could she ask to speak with the chef? Somehow, that did not sit too well with her. One does not go up to the front door of a grand residence and request to have a word with the chef, does one? Perhaps, she ought to go round and call in at the servant's entrance—Heaven's no! That would be shocking indeed! Not the thing at all for a lady!

Besides, she did not even know the chef's name! To Pamela's thinking, the problem was quickly growing as insurmountable as it had ever been. She sighed and shook her head.

For a time she did not stir, concentrating all her powers upon the problem. It seemed to her that Mr. Euclid did not have all the answers, by far.

Finally she sighed. It was not something that she could plan. If she would pursue the matter, she would just have to go out to the duke's house and speak to whomever she could. If it turned out to be his Grace, then so be it. Surely, if his Grace was dissatisfied with his chef, he would not begrudge her an opportunity to interview the fellow—or, at the very least, to arrange for him to call upon her at her home. Pamela was now thinking that, once she had got her man into the Pollworth's home, her ladyship might be sufficiently exercised over the matter to make a stand with her father. It was a pale hope, but for the moment, it was all she could muster.

Although the Great Frost had abated, it was a chilly morning that afforded Pamela the opportunity to embark upon her little adventure. Lady Pollworth had opened her eyes that day and sleepily inquired of her maid as to the weather. Upon being informed that, despite a few degrees of frost, it was quite cheery, she had let out a groan, requested that her breakfast be brought to her, and settled back in her bed, saying: "Take my compliments to your master and inform him that I shall be pleased to come down when the spring has returned, and not a day sooner."

Pamela went up to speak with her ladyship, found there was nothing but a winter's ennui disturbing her mother, and came down to have breakfast with her father.

In the breakfast room, she was met with an apology from her sire for having to go right off to the City. Urgent matters called him there. He had himself a sip of coffee, planted a kiss upon her cheek, begged her to relay his farewell to her mother, and rushed out.

For a little while at least, Pamela was to be quite the mistress of the house. She sat down to table, and Gibbs served her a hearty breakfast.

"Gibbs, what have you heard regarding our illustrious neighbors?"

"I beg your pardon, Miss Pamela, but I am not sure to whom you are referring. If I may say so, all the neighboring families about the Square are quite distinguished, quite a bit more so than was the case at Clandon Park."

"Yes, I quite agree, but I have reference to the Duke of Pevensey. I looked him up in *Debrett's* this morning and discovered that his house is situate in Bloomsbury Square. Mecklenburg can only boast an earl, so we are quite put in the shade."

"Ah, the Duke of Pevensey. Yes, Miss Pamela, I have heard it mentioned, but I pray you will forgive me. We have been so occupied with arranging this place that I have not had a chance to sample the local gossip," he said with a smile. "Will there be anything else, Miss Pamela?"

"No, I think not. I shall be going out for a bit in a little while. If my lady asks for me, I shall be back anon. I am just going for a stroll about the Square."

"Very good, miss."

Pamela had difficulty hiding her exultation at having found the duke's direction, more especially because it had turned out to be so close by. She would have no need of a carriage to get there, nor would it be at all exceptional for her to be out alone, as it was right in her very own neighborhood. She had her wraps fetched and left the house.

Compared to what it had been, the weather was mild. Although one could see one's breath, cheeks and noses were in no danger of painful nips. And that was a good thing, for it turned out that Bloomsbury Square was at a greater distance than Pamela had imagined.

It was Russell Square that she came to and mistook for her destination. It was a very large place, quite adequate in her opinion to accommodate a duke. Upon inquiry of a governess, out with her charges, she discovered that she still had almost as far to go as she had already come.

When she finally did arrive in Bloomsbury Square, she was very surprised to see that it was barely as large as Mecklenburg. But, as the houses facing upon it were quite grand, she was sure that some of them, at least, were suited for a duke.

A passing tradesman pointed Pevensey House out to her, and she strolled over to it, to stand before the great structure while she came to a decision as to how she ought to proceed. Now that she had arrived, it was not an easy thing to go up to the door and pursue her inquiry. She was very much aware that even a married lady would have felt out of place at this point.

But she had given so much thought to the business and, now, had come so far with it, she could not contemplate a retreat before she had made the attempt. With her heart in her mouth, she went up to the door, raised the silver knocker, and let it fall twice.

The door slowly opened and a footman appeared. But what a footman he was! Pamela had never seen such a tall person. He towered over her, and there was a supercilious look upon his countenance as he stared down at her. The powder upon the tremendous wig he sported had all the appearance of a snow-covered haystack and made him look that much taller. His manner was as frosty as his wig as he said, in a sonorous tone: "The Duchess of Pevensey is not to be disturbed at this hour, madam. Is there a message?"

"Oh, it is not the duchess I wish to speak with, my good man—" she could not continue, because the footman's features were undergoing a drastic change. His head was now bent to study her, instead of staring out into the street. "You have come to call upon his Grace. I beg your pardon, madam, but I have not been informed that he is expecting anyone—"

"No, it is not the duke I wish to see. It is the chef. Would you happen to know his name?"

The footman stared at her, his features grown puffy. The arrogant expression in his face had now given way to a look of horror. Even his faultless livery seemed to be shrinking with aversion, for where there had been a smooth expanse of silken brocade across his chest, it was now wrinkled and showing signs of strain as his Eminence fought to maintain his adamantine demeanor.

Pamela was frightened. She knew for a certainty, now, her undertaking was in very poor taste and wished that she had never started it. In an unconscious gesture, she crossed her arms across her breast and was about to turn away when the shattered footman, having found his voice, gave vent to a Vesuvian outburst.

"Hippolyte! It is Galliard you want? How dare that insufferable French pig summon his baggage to the front door of this house! Go away with you!" he cried, waving her off. Then he drew himself erect and resumed his lost eminence, tugging smartly down at his lapels. Believing that he was now fully restored to his accustomed imposing grandeur, he turned solemnly about, stepped inside, and slammed the door shut in Pamela's face.

She stood aghast, completely at a loss how to proceed. The footman's insulting behavior had thoroughly crushed her.

She turned about and started to leave. Then she paused and turned back. The fellow had been insufferable! As a lady, she must resent his manner. It behooved her to go over his head, and she raised her hand and rapped the knocker sharply on the door.

Again it began to open slowly. She dived into her reticule and snatched out of it her card. Holding it up before her, she thrust it into the footman's face before he could utter a word.

"I demand to see his Grace. Never in my life have I been so humiliated. My card, fellow!"

By this time, the liveried lout was puffing and blowing. Wave upon wrinkled wave ruffled his shirtfront as he bent over to read the tiny square, fumbling for a be-ribboned eyeglass to aid his sight. His neckcloth became a veritable ruin as his gaping jaw crushed down upon it.

"B-but, my dear Miss Pollworth, you never said—I mean to say it was Hippolyte you—Oh, I pray that I did not offend you, Miss Pollworth, beyond all forgiveness. His Grace can be very hard."

All the cold, haughtiness of his tone and bearing were now quite dissipated, and Pamela began to fear that the huge fellow was about to break into tears as he lamented: "I pray you, Miss Pollworth—I mean to say it is something quite unusual for a lady to come to inquire for our chef. What was I to think? What was I to do?"

He stared at her dazedly, not knowing what to say next. For her part, Pamela was at a loss to know how to go on, she had no wish to speak with the duke. That was for her parents to do, if it were to prove necessary. She only had this wish to talk with Hippolyte. Considering the utter ruin this desire of hers had brought to the duke's footman, things were looking most discouraging.

But, she had to do something, and the footman was

61

rendered completely useless for the time being. Whatever was to follow, it was up to her to begin it.

"How are you called, my good man?" she asked, thinking that this was an excellent way to begin.

"I am Twemlow, Jonathan Twemlow an it please you, Miss Pollworth."

"Yes, Twemlow. I do believe that we can pass over this unpleasantness. Possibly, I ought not to have asked for your chef before I had had a word with his Grace. All things considered, if his Grace will receive on such short notice, I should be greatly pleased, of course; but if his Grace is too occupied and has no objection, I should be pleased to speak with Monsieur Galliard."

Twemlow shuddered and asked: "Er—Miss Pollworth, is that the message you wish me to take in to his Grace?"

"Yes, I think that will do—Oh! do not forget my card! Here!"

Twemlow took it between the tips of his gloved fingers, stepped back and bowed Pamela into the entrance hall. He, then, excused himself and went off in search of his master, fussing with his livery with one hand, while the other held the card out before him as though he were a herald about to deliver a flag of truce.

Chapter V

As Pamela stepped within, she forgot about Twemlow and his message. All her attention was taken up by her surroundings. She had known that the house was much larger than her own, but that had not impressed her. A ducal residence was bound to be something grander and something finer than that of a mere baron. What was quite taking her breath away was the scale of the great entrance hall and the exquisite mode of its adornment.

It was all done up in white and gold. Upon each wall was a great mirror, and facing her across the great expanse was a broad but graceful staircase, each step cushioned in what appeared to be a velvety red. It was enchanting, and she could hardly believe that it was but the entrance hall.

Along each of the three walls, centered under each huge, gilt-framed mirror, was a long divan, richly upholstered in silk, each in a different color. There was a blue divan, a yellow divan and a red divan. Between each divan, was a great door, only the one through which Twemlow had disappeared, standing ajar.

She walked slowly over to the staircase and felt the glowing, smooth wood of the railing. She took the first step and then the second, the soft cushions giving her a pleasurable sensation.

On the third step, she turned and curtsied to an imaginary assemblage below her, smiling charmingly all the while.

But there was a witness to her little drama and he, laughingly, bowed back to her. Then, he came forward and took her by the hand, leading her down to the floor of the hall, saying: "How very lovely, my dear. I am sure that staircase was built just for you, it takes to you so well."

Pamela was blushing in her confusion and embarrassment. She began to stammer her apologies, trying to explain her errand, and at the same time, scrutinizing the intruder with great care.

He was not so tall. But he was taller than she. After Twemlow, every one was bound to appear to have shrunk. He was young, but older than she, and he had the nicest brown, wavy hair. His smile was sweet, too, and there were no airs about him. She calculated that he must be some sort of secretary to the duke. His clothes would not allow of much more, for he was wearing a shabby coat, a simple neckband, and his linen was in need of a change. She thought that the duke was not overly particular with regard to the neatness of those who served him.

He seemed to read her mind, for he said: "I pray you will pardon my appearance. I should have changed sooner had I known we were to entertain so charming a lady. Are you calling on her Grace? I am sure I do not number you amongst my acquaintances, or I should have known you, in an instant."

Pamela could not help blushing. He was very nice, she thought, but he seemed to be rather presumptuous.

"Thank you, sir, but I have business with his Grace and am waiting to learn if he will see me."

The young man's eyebrows went up. "Oh, I think that he will see you. Never fear, Miss—or is it Mrs.?"

"I am Miss Pollworth. Pray do not stand upon ceremony. If you have something to do, there is not the slightest need for you to entertain me."

"Oh, I do not mind. I have nothing more important to do at the moment, Miss Pollworth. It would give me great pleasure to see you entertained. May I inquire what is your business with the duke?"

Pamela frowned. It was bound to be a bit troublesome to explain that it was the duke's chef she actually wished to have a word with. Besides, it was no business of his and hardly, as she saw it, of the duke's either.

"I should prefer to keep that between his Grace and myself, if you please."

He shrugged. "As you wish, my dear. Why do you not sit down? If I know Twemlow, he will be forever finding his Grace."

As Pamela took her seat on the red divan, he sat down, or rather lolled, upon the yellow. There was such a careless air about him that Pamela began to suspect he might be of some greater importance in the household. On a venture, she inquired: "Sir, you are not the marquess by any chance, are you?"

He grinned at her and shook his head. "No, my

65

dear, I am not the marquess by any chance at all. I say, Twemlow is taking a bit longer than usual to find the duke, don't you think?"

"I really cannot say. I have met Twemlow but this once, sir."

"Ah. Do you happen to reside in Bloomsbury? I should hardly think so, or I should have made it a point of calling upon you."

Pamela thought he had a great nerve to say anything of the sort. "I am sure I am flattered, sir. As it happens, I dwell in Mecklenburg Square—"

"How terribly nice!" he exclaimed, sitting up and beginning to study her. "In Mecklenburg, is it? How could I have missed you?"

"Perhaps it is because my father, Lord Pollworth, has taken a house there and we have removed from Surrey but a month ago."

"Have you really! What a shame! I wish to assure you that this odious frost we have just got over is not at all characteristic of London's climate."

"I should think not! The cold has invested the entire kingdom and the newspapers are full of it!"

"You read the newspapers, do you?"

"Is that in any way exceptional?"

"Hardly. I find it most refreshing in a female. It might prove a treat if we were to have ourselves a little discussion about the day's events."

Pamela was finding him very attractive, and this disturbed her. She had heard many tales of the rakes of London. If ever a fellow fit that description, she was inclined to believe that her present company did so to a T. He was too charming, by far, to be sincere.

She replied: "It might, but not to me. My brother has come down from Oxford, and we hold many an intelligent conversation. He is quite learned, you see."

"I do indeed. It was three years ago that I came down from Cambridge. I should like to meet this brother of yours."

Pamela complimented herself on her judgment. She had been right from the first. He was the duke's secretary. It was just the sort of post that Geoffrey was seeking, with his bachelor's degree.

At that moment, Twemlow made his appearance. He was looking very troubled as he came into the hall from one of the other doors. Upon spying the young man, he exclaimed: "Ah, there you are, your Grace. I have been looking all over for you—Oh dear, you have already met the lady, for you are speaking with her—"

"Yes, Twemlow. You have found me. Please show Miss Pollworth into the drawing room whilst I go and change into something more respectable, and pray inform her Grace that we have company. I think she will be interested to meet Miss Pollworth."

"Very good, your Grace," said Twemlow, retiring through the door he had just come through.

In an instant he was back into the hall again, all apologies as he marched over to the first door and went out.

Pamela was staring at the duke, her mind a perfect jumble of confusion. He could not be the duke, he was too young! Heavens, what a sight she must look! She had never meant to speak with a duke, especially not one so young and handsome! What must he think of her!

Then came the thought to sweep every other one aside: For gracious sakes, why do I continue to sit upon the divan like a frozen goose? If he is the duke—and I am sure that he is—I must make my duty to him!

She arose abruptly, just as his Grace had come over

to her, and sank into a curtsy. "I beg your pardon, your Grace, but I did not recognize you. You were not at all in the attire of a duke."

As she said it, she blushed. It was an awfully stupid remark.

The duke laughed as he took her by the hand and bid her rise. "Had I known you were coming, my dear Miss Pollworth, I assure you, I should have donned every bit of my regalia so that you could not have mistaken me. Perhaps, now you will be kind enough to inform me of the purpose of your visit?"

"I beg your pardon, your Grace. If I had but known it was you—but you are so young. I should never have thought that you were junior to my father in years!"

"Nor should I. It would be a wonder of the world if he were younger than I and yet could boast such a lovely daughter as you, my dear."

"But I looked you up in *Debrett's* and I was sure it said that you were born in 1764—Oh dear, you must have been the marquess then! How terribly silly of me not to have realized that you had succeeded your late father."

"Never fret. My lady mother, now Dowager, has the same difficulty. In her eyes, I am still the marquess—and that, purely by courtesy."

"I am sure you must find that quite trying, your Grace. But now, I must be running along—"

"Oh, I pray you will stay, Miss Pollworth. A little longer, at least. I would have you meet my mother as long as you are here—"

As far as Pamela was concerned, she had had enough of the entire undertaking. It had gotten completely out of hand, and she was sure that she would never hear the end of it from either of her parents—if they came to learn of this outing of hers. She quickly interrupted the duke.

"It is too kind of you, your Grace, but I have been out for too long as it is. I am sure I should be delighted to meet the duchess at another more propitious time—"

"Nonsense! Why, we have not even been properly introduced, and we have been talking together all of twenty minutes, I do believe. Come, Miss Pollworth, today, up to the moment I espied you, has been a dreadful bore. I know that my mother would enjoy meeting a new neighbor."

"H-how are you called, your Grace?"

"That's better! I have the pleasure and the honor of being—I say, is it the entire litany you wish to hear?"

Pamela did not understand and looked a question at him.

He made a small bow and declared: "I have the honor of being Gerald John Frederick, Duke of Pevensey, Marquess of Falhurst, Earl of Stokes and of Tainsley. To my friends, I am Gerald, and the name of my family is Lytton—but I am sure you must know all this, if you have referred to the *Peerage*."

"Then you were the Marquess of Falhurst before?"

"Yes, and that will be the style of my eldest son, when I have got one." He chuckled. "But, of course, all that must wait upon my marriage, Miss Pollworth. May I inquire how you are called? I, too, could go to *Debrett's*, but I am sure you will want to save me the trouble."

Pamela was feeling rather shy. She wished she could refuse him, not that she was not enjoying the conversation. It was only that she felt that she was in deep water and wished to bring the business to an end. She could hardly tell him what the purpose of her visit had been, and she was very worried lest Twemlow might inform his Grace of the conversation he had held with her. It would be too, too embarrassing if it ever came to the duke's knowledge.

Still, she saw no way of bringing this little meeting to an end, and admitted to herself that she really did not wish to.

She smiled and replied: "My litany is a deal shorter than yours. I am the Honorable Pamela Pollworth, only daughter to Frederick Lord Pollworth, of Clandon Park, Surrey. We have, but recently, taken up residence at No. 18 Mecklenburg Square; so you see it was but a short walk to Bloomsbury Square."

"How very nice that is! Very convenient, indeed," remarked the duke. "But I say, do sit down—or better yet, let me send to her Grace. We could, all three, sit down to a cup of tea—"

"Thank you, your Grace, but I ought to be leaving. I am sure that I am intruding—"

"Not at all! Not at all, Miss Pamela. Come! I shall brook no denial," he said, and he reached over to the bellrope.

At once, Twemlow made his appearance. The duke conferred a slightly sour look upon him, and then ordered a collation to be prepared. "And where, may I ask, is Plunkett?"

"It was just that I had happened by, your Grace, else I am sure that Mr. Plunkett must have responded. Ah, here he is now!"

The butler had just entered the hall. He looked to his Grace for instruction, while he raised an eyebrow at Twemlow. That worthy immediately decamped on the errand the duke had given him, and Plunkett shook his head despairingly.

"I must apologize, your Grace, for Twemlow. He is a bit of an old woman—"

"Never mind—but I do often wonder how he can manage to fold up that great height of his in order to get his ear to the keyhole.

"Enough. Present my compliments to her Grace, with the request that she assist me in entertaining a most charming new neighbor. I have sent Twemlow to Hippolyte to arrange a collation. Pray look into the business as I am sure that our illustrious chef will have some remark to pass. I do not think that Twemlow is any match for him."

A tiny smile lighted Plunkett's face. He bowed and said: "At once, your Grace."

All of this time, he had not cast one look in Pamela's direction, but now, as he departed, he looked intently at her as he went out of the room.

His Grace smiled and remarked: "I do believe that Plunkett approves, my dear. He can usually mask his curiosity completely."

"Mama, it is the most fortunate thing!" exclaimed the duke as he ushered Pamela into a room that was smaller and cozier than the many great ones they had passed through. "Miss Pamela Pollworth is the daughter of our neighbor in Mecklenburg Square. Lord Pollworth and his family have taken residence there but recently. I expect that we shall be seeing something of them in the not too distant future."

The Dowager was seated in an easy chair by the window, facing into the room. She nodded, as Pamela curtsied to her, and said: "Those houses are selling so quickly, one would think that were being given away. Of course, any family situated in Mecklenburg *must* be a recent arrival, your Grace. I wish you would not present the obvious to me."

71

"I shall try to remember, Mama," he said, in a submissive tone.

The Dowager looked quizzically at him, and replied: "You always say so, but you never do. What are you waiting for, your Grace? Offer the girl a chair!"

"My pleasure, madam," he said. As he brought up a chair for Pamela, he murmured: "She's a veritable dragon, you know; but do not let her put it over you. Actually, she is quite harmless."

"I heard that, your Grace!" exclaimed the duchess. "To think it is my own child who speaks so against his own mother. I may be a dragon but you, pet, are a serpent's tooth!"

If Pamela had been uncomfortable at the prospect of meeting the duchess before, now that it had become a reality, her uneasiness had multiplied. The Dowager appeared to her as a fearsome lady, and it shocked her that, for all his Grace's apparent submissiveness, the cheery smile on his lips had not faded, nor did he give the slightest indication of respect for his mother. On the other hand, as he was a duke, it was the strangest thing to hear her Grace continually address him as "your Grace" but in tones that held no regard for his exalted rank. It was beyond her understanding how mother and son managed to get on together; yet, of all who were in the room at the moment, she, herself, was the only one who was ill-at-ease.

It did not make matters any easier for her, when the duchess exclaimed: "Now, your Grace, I do believe we have managed to frighten the pretty little creature!"

"Oh, then I do apologize, first, to Miss Pollworth and, second, to you, Mama—"

"You have your nerve, your Grace! I should think I take precedence over the young lady!"

It startled Pamela to think that now they were about to argue over her. She stammered: "I have no wish to become the cause of a family argument—"

"It is quite all right, Miss Pamela. Mother is only funning. I do not think she comprehends the light in the distant future—perhaps."

At that remark, both the Lady Charlotte and Pamela looked askance at the duke.

"Gerald, I am not sure what you intend with that remark, but I strongly suspect it is to my discomfiture."

He laughed. "I think not, Mama, but time will tell. In the meantime, I am of the opinion that we are treating our guest most miserably. She is convinced that we are at each other's throats."

Pamela let out a slow breath. It was nothing as bad as she had been thinking. But she gasped and turned to the duchess, as that lady inquired, rather sharply: "So you are in Mecklenburg Square, are you? I have not been out that way for months. I did not like what they were doing then, and I am sure I shall not like what they are doing to the place now. Those dear orphans in the Foundling Home must be in the poorest circumstances, their vistas all cluttered up with homes, such as *they* have never known. I cannot understand why any one in his right mind should ever wish to live outside of Bloomsbury!"

"I beg your pardon, Mama, but I must point out that Mecklenburg Square is included in Bloomsbury," said the Duke.

"Nonsense! It cannot be, or I should have known it!" retorted her Grace.

"Nonetheless, it is true, my dear. Mecklenburg has become a part of Bloomsbury."

"Is that a fact? Then, I dare say, the Pollworths are neighbors to us in truth."

"Now you have got it, madam!" cried the duke, laughing.

"Truly, Gerald, you are too old to be making such a fuss over this nonsense. Miss Pollworth shows a deal more sense than do you. See, she does not find anything funny at all. My dear, you must have Lady Pollworth pay me a call soon." This to Pamela.

"Thank you, your Grace. My lady mother will be honored to do so."

"Spoken like a well-bred young lady!" said her Grace, approvingly.

"Ah, here comes Plunkett with refreshments!" she said as the butler wheeled in a serving cart, loaded with the makings of tea. "I pray that Hippolyte made no difficulty about this," she added, looking at Plunkett.

Plunkett paused in his serving to say: "I fear, your Grace, that it was the usual thing."

He coughed slightly behind his hand and added: "I was put to the trouble of rescuing Twemlow. He does not get on too well with Monsieur Galliard."

"What news this time, Plunkett?" asked the duke, grinning. "Was it with his great knife or his cleaver that he went after Twemlow?"

Sadly, Plunkett announced: "It was the former, your Grace," at which the duke burst into hearty laughter.

Pamela was very puzzled. As she had heard that the duke and his chef were on the outs with each other, she was at a loss to understand his Grace's laughter.

"Truly, your Grace, it is a shame the way you encourage that French savage," admonished the duchess. "One would think that Hippolyte was the only French chef in creation."

"With regard to his talent for the cuisine of his

native land, you are quite correct. I would not part with him for any amount. He is priceless."

Now Pamela understood precisely how foolhardy she had been. She thanked her stars that she had not let out the purpose of her visit to the duke, and was more than ever eager to remove herself from Pevensey House.

"I pray you will excuse me, your Graces, but I must be getting on home. It has been a most pleasant visit, and I shall inform my mother of your wish, your Grace."

"Oh, but you cannot go! Not until you inform me of the reason behind this call of yours, my dear. Remember, you said it was only to the duke that you would reveal it. Now that you know I am the duke, I pray you will feel free to tell me about it. I assure you I am most interested. If there is something I can do for you, you have but to name it."

"Oh, you are kindness itself, your Grace! As to *that* business, it truly was not all that important and I should prefer to forget it, if you do not mind."

"Oh, but I do mind, and very much, too! What brought you to my door?"

"I—I'd rather not say. Truly it is not of the least importance."

"Why do you not let me be the judge of that, my dear?"

"Gerald, behave yourself, and let the poor girl alone," scolded the duchess. "If Miss Pollworth has had second thoughts—and now that she has seen what an addlewit you are, I do not blame her in the least—you must respect her wish in the matter."

"Of course, Mama. As always, you are right. Then, I suppose it would be ill-mannered of me to insist upon your staying, Miss Pollworth. You have your carriage and maid awaiting you, of course. I shall be pleased to see you out."

"Now that is more like, Gerald. I have hopes for you, not many, but you just may turn out to be the duke your father was," remarked the duchess, as she smiled at Pamela.

It was more than Pamela's poor head could comprehend. Mother and son were forever bickering with each other; yet, neither of them was put out of humor by any of it.

She stood up and said: "I thank you very much, your Grace, but that will not be necessary. I am sure that I can find my way out. In any case, I have come quite unescorted, it was such a very little distance. I shall be quite able to walk back to Mecklenburg Square."

"I would not hear of it! It is quite a piece. Nonsense! I shall drive you home myself. Plunkett, have my curricle got ready. Twemlow can act as my tiger."

Plunkett looked aghast. "Did you say, Twemlow, your Grace?"

"I said Twemlow, Plunkett. I admit he is something large for a tiger but I have not got anyone else. Perhaps, we can go by the Home and find a young chap willing to don my livery. I say, Miss Pollworth, would you mind very much if we stopped at the Home and interviewed one or two of the little chaps? We just might be fortunate enough to find a tad who is something familiar with horses."

As Pamela had not the vaguest idea of what he was saying, she blindly nodded.

"Am I to understand that as 'yes, you do mind,' or is it 'yes, it would be quite all right'?"

"Just a moment, your Grace, there is something in

all of this I am not sure that I approve," intervened the duchess.

Both Pamela and the duke looked at her.

"How comes it that a young lady, who I am sure has all the advantages, is permitted to go about without a maid and footman, without any escort at all? My dear Miss Pollworth, I find it difficult to believe that Lady Pollworth, if she is any sort of mother, would have allowed it."

Oh, if only she could have got away earlier, thought Pamela. Now, it must of a certainty get back to her mother that she had gone about the city, unattended.

"I had just gone out for a bit of a stroll. I had heard mention of the Duke of Pevensey and thought to inquire—as any good neighbor ought. It is not thought exceptional in Surrey to call upon one's neighbors, your Grace."

"Now do not try to come it over me, young lady! That will not wash! There had to be some other reason for you to venture forth in such a desperate fashion."

Pamela was at a loss for words. She was very much embarrassed and the high color in her cheeks showed it.

"Yes, I was thinking it was deucedly odd, too," remarked the duke. Then he smiled and went on. "But, as you have said, Mama, it is Miss Pamela's business to decide to inform us or not to as she pleases. We have no business to natter at her in this highly irregular manner."

"I do declare, Gerald, I do not consider my conversation nattering!" exploded the duchess.

"One never does, does one?" he retorted with a grin, and the duchess burst into merry laughter. "Ah yes," she said, "one day, when you are not about, I shall press Miss Pollworth in my own inimitable way to reveal to me how she came to make this call on us. For the nonce, see her home, dear boy, and carry my compliments to Lord and Lady Pollworth. They have a lovely if somewhat puzzling girl for a daughter—but we shall get to the bottom of it, eventually, I promise you."

Chapter VI

Pamela was greatly relieved to find herself free of the trying conversation, but not completely. It seemed that the Duke of Pevensey had an eye for the ridiculous. If she thought to return home in his curricle, attracting little attention, she was greatly mistaken.

The excessively tall and full-fleshed footman, his face screwed into a sour expression, took up what might have been the usual post of a footman attending his master in a carriage. In this case, the curricle was quite a small vehicle as compared to a coach, and when Twemlow stepped up behind, he quite towered over the equipage, giving it a most comical appearance. One glance at him, trying to hold his great bulk fast to the little carriage, and she understood what his Grace meant by a tiger. It would, naturally, be a small boy, dressed in livery, in place of Twemlow, and that was why they were on their way to the Foundling Home, to find his replacement.

Pamela marveled at the way her venture into Bloomsbury Square was turning out. She had set forth, the procurement of a chef for her family's kitchen her only concern, and now, some three hours later, she was in the strangest sort of pickle, very much sans chef. Except for the fact that the duke was chattering away, with never a pause, it could have been a most disappointing time for her.

She peered out at his Grace from the corner of her eye and noted, once again, that he was a quite handsome gentleman, and not at all her picture of what a duke ought to look like. He was far too young for that role, she thought, and smiled to herself. Apparently the duchess felt that way, too.

Perhaps, if he had not been so charming, she would have given serious thought to what was in store for her when she finally arrived home; but it did not appear that she would be getting to Mecklenburg Square, until his Grace had made his call at the Coram Hospital for Foundlings, whose grounds were situated along the opposite side of the square in which she dwelt. Even now, as they were approaching it, the duke was prattling on.

". . . so you see, I was on my way out for the purpose of coming here, when I encountered you in the hall. It is a rather new institution, having been erected about 1750. Oddly enough, its founder, Captain Coram, was not a man of means, but he was a man of benevolence. The place owes much of its character to him, I believe. The orphans are very well taken care of, and we see to it that it is maintained to their advantage.

"Since, as you can see, from that excrescence of a Twemlow, who is hanging on for dear life behind, I am in sore need of a tiger—what better place than this?"

"What *is* a tiger, your Grace?" asked Pamela.

"Have you none such in Surrey?"

"Not that I know of, but then the gentlemen out there, who ride about in these 'flimsy flytraps,' as my father refers to them, are usually at racing with each other all the time, and they load their vehicles as lightly as possible."

"Flimsy flytrap, is it! I suspect your father is a gentleman of the old school. Nothing but solid weight in a vehicle for him. I should venture to guess that he is a Tory into the bargain."

"Oh yes, that he is. Are you?"

"I have not made up my mind. For that matter, I have not attended many sessions at the Lords for that very reason. There are so many sides to every question that is presented, I marvel that *anyone* can decide which is the right one.

"But, to answer your question, a tiger is actually a miniature version of a footman. He has to be tiny to go with these tiny carriages, you see; so it is a deal easier to find oneself a young chap who can handle a horse, than to try to find a dwarf. Of course, the best sort are older coves who have not grown to any great height and weight, but they, too, are not easy to find. In any case, one has to go cautiously, as there is a degree of informality between a man and his tiger. Insolence in a little boy can be excused, even laughed at, but never in an older chap."

"I see. But why do you call such a little fellow a tiger?"

"I really can't say. It is something new, you see. I suppose one might call, having a tiger, something of an affectation. Perhaps it is to distinguish the little groom from a page, but why a tiger, I have not the vaguest idea. If it were not for these curricles that are constructed so 'flimsily' as your father might say, and with so little room behind for a proper-sized fellow, I doubt if there ever would have been a need for 'em."

At this point they had driven onto the grounds of the hospital, and were approaching the front portal. They drew to a stop and Twemlow, looking rather pale, came round to take the horses' heads.

"You will come in with me, will you not?" asked his Grace.

Pamela smiled and nodded. He helped her out of the curricle, and together, they went up to the door, which was now standing open, its edge decorated by the heads of two small boys looking out at them, their eyes filled with curiosity and hope.

Pamela had heard terrible tales of what went on behind the walls of orphanages all her life, but it was quite obvious that the Coram Hospital was not in the general run of such institutions. The little inmates appeared to be in blooming good health, and they had as well scrubbed an appearance as did the place itself. In fact, the hospital was an impressive place on any count.

There were ample grounds about it and the structure was of a rather attractive styling, being quite in line with the residences on the other sides of the square. There were gardens and a playground for the children with grass plots and gravel walks all about. The interior was even more of a surprise to Pamela, for it was richly decorated with excellent paintings by eminent painters, such as Hogarth and West, obviously donated by the wealthy friends of this charity. Pamela was pleased to know that his Grace was one of the benefactors. It spoke well of him.

The duke had sent a message on before him, with

the result that a small group of boys was assembled for his inspection. There was such a look of desperate eagerness in their eyes it quite broke Pamela's heart that only one of them could be selected for the post.

The duke was very kind in his manner as he spoke to each of them, handing out pieces of silver at the end of each little conversation. Finally, with a sigh and the remark: "I wish I could take all of them," he settled upon a sprightly lad of ten and sent him out to wait with Twemlow at the curricle.

There were generous compliments all about as his Grace put his signature to the lad's articles, while Pamela was hard-pressed to restrain her tears at the scene.

The duke then escorted Pamela back to the curricle, and they were in time to witness the new tiger, resplendent in the scarlet livery of the orphanage, making a hash of Twemlow's silk stockings with the toes of his boots. His great height seemed to be a distinct disadvantage to the footman as he clumsily tried to fend off the little monster with no success at all. Pamela blushed to hear the very profane war cries of the two ill-matched combatants that were filling the air.

"Here, now, what the devil is going on?" demanded the duke. "Twemlow, I am ashamed of you! Is that any way for a footman to behave?"

Twemlow finally managed to get the palm of his hand set upon the head of the new tiger, so that the latter was unable to press home his attack—although, he never ceased trying, kicking out into the empty air with his feet.

"Your Grace, my humble apologies, but this beastly little vermin insists he is going to ride in your Grace's carriage. I had assumed that it was what you have selected to be your tiger, and I was merely attempting to convince it that its place would be up behind."

"Boy! Herbert, I bid you desist at once!" snapped the duke.

Herbert turned from Twemlow and regarded his Grace with a snuffle.

" 'Erbert be me nyme, yer Gryce, an' I don' think much o' this longshanks, I don't! 'E's a queer 'un, 'e is!"

"That is precisely how I addressed you, Herbert—"

"Nah! Nah! There ye go again, Mister duke, yer Gryce. Ye did the syme in 'orspital! 'T bean't Huh-'erbert! It be 'Erbert, yer lordship!" explained 'Erbert, vociferously, even a bit belligerently.

"Hmm," mused the duke. "Perhaps we can reach a compromise. If you are going to stay with me, I shall call you Bertie—"

"Bertie? Me nyme ain't *Bertie!*" protested 'Erbert, with anger.

"Now, look you, young man! You are being too impertinent by far! I have a mind to turn you back to the hospital and find me another, better behaved, little man for my tiger."

Twemlow reached out and took hold of 'Erbert's ear. "It will be my pleasure, your Grace."

"Aiyeow!!" screamed the little cherub, grabbing at Twemlow's great hand with both of his.

Pamela, quite forgetting herself in the pathos of the moment, cried out: "Twemlow, you brute, unhand the boy!!"

Twemlow gave a start and loosed his grip. At once, 'Erbert rushed up to Pamela and clutched at her knees: "Oh, yer lydy Gryce, ye'll not 'low them nasty coves to put me back in 'Orspital! Yer kin call me anythin' ye want, only don' 'low them chaps ter put me back in

84

'Orspital!!" and he fell to bawling and hiding his now grubby little face in her skirts.

Pamela placed a soft hand upon his head and looked, pleadingly at the duke. "You are not going to take him back there, are you, your Grace?"

From the depths of his despair, 'Erbert let loose a harangue: "No, no! Le' me be! They be nasty ones! I be whipped an' beat an' starved, an' I shall run awy fro' them!"

"Hush, you little beast!" cried the duke. "And unhand the lady, for goodness sake! All right, I shan't turn you back this time, but you had better be on your best behavior and do what you are told, do you hear? I shall not stand for you going about massacring my servants.

"You are to be my tiger and your place will be up behind this carriage. Furthermore, you will watch over the horses when we are out together, and you will assist in the stables at other times. For this, you shall be attired in livery and have a bob a week for your pocket, a place to sleep, and enough to fill your stomach. But I caution you Bertie, no more whoppers. Not a one, do you hear? I know the hospital better than you and nothing of the sort which you describe goes on there. Look at you, red-cheeked and plump as a partridge, and do not try to come it over me!"

Bertie was grinning with satisfaction as he got up off his knees and wiped his nose on his sleeve.

Twemlow turned away in disgust as the duke looked at Pamela and said: "I suspect that I am inheriting Pandora's reticule in Bertie, and I have you to thank for it, my dear."

"Oh, but he is such an adorable little tyke!" she replied.

He chuckled. "That is not quite how *I* should have described him."

He handed her into the carriage and turned to Twemlow. "I do not trust the youngster to be able to hold onto his station behind until he has had some training. The carriage is too small to carry all of us, so you had better stay with him, here, until I come by for you. I have a wish to speak with you. Until I return, you might get to know the little monster and try to give him some idea of how he is to comport himself in my service—and I bid you do it in a kindly fashion. I do not think that his having been brought up in a foundling home, even the best of them, can have given him any great notion of the ways of the fashionable world."

"Very good, your Grace. I shall do my best."

Pamela invited his Grace to come in with her to meet her father and mother, but the duke begged off, explaining that he was not dressed for the occasion, and furthermore, he did not wish to leave Twemlow and Bertie alone together for longer than it was absolutely necessary. Good footmen were hard to come by, he explained with a laugh.

Pamela thanked him for all his kindness and he saw her to her door.

"Great heavens, Pamela, where on earth have you been? You disappeared without a word to anyone, and when I came down this morning, it was as though I had never had a daughter!" cried Lady Pollworth, as Pamela came into the sitting room.

Pamela let out a little laugh and flung her hat onto a chair in the corner. Then she came over to her mother and planted a light kiss upon her ladyship's brow.

As she sat down opposite, she said, cheerily: "Mama, I have had the strangest adventure!"

"Did you? Then I do not have to tell you that that is what happens to young ladies who go about the streets all by themselves. Truly, my dear, you have got to remember that this is not Surrey. It is most exceptional for you to appear anywhere in London without an escort. Oh, I pray you did not venture so far as Covent Garden. I hear that that is a most disreputable district."

"Never as far as all that! I merely went for a stroll about Bloomsbury. Have you ever been in Bloomsbury Square?"

"I cannot say that I have. You know how busy I have been plotting and planning how we shall present ourselves to our neighbors," her ladyship explained as she put down the penny-romance she had been diligently studying when Pamela came in.

"So I see—and I can assure you that I have had an adventure which, by comparison, makes pale what *you* have been reading."

Lady Pollworth smiled a superior smile. "I am sure you have. Bloomsbury is quite the most romantic place in the kingdom," she said, drily.

"You *would* think so if you only knew who I met," countered her daughter.

"A young gentleman, I do not doubt. And that is what comes of your having been out all by yourself. A lady is not safe on the streets of the city these days."

"I was brought home by the Duke of Pevensey, himself, and—"

Lady Pollworth burst into laughter. "The Duke of Pevensey? Oh, my dear, I thought you had grown out of your reveries and daydreams. In any case, I do not see why you should have picked on the Duke of Pevensey. He is a number of years older than your father, if I remember correctly. We looked the gentleman up in *Debrett's*."

"Oh, but that duke is dead, Mama, and—"

"All the more reason for you not to have fancies about him. I say let him rest in peace."

"Oh, Mama, it is nothing at all like that. It was the young duke, his son who succeeded him. Our *Debrett's* is something out-of-date for he has been the duke for some years."

"Who has?"

"The marquess, of course, except that now he is the duke—and he was kind enough to take me home."

Lady Pollworth was frowning now. "Do you mean to tell me that a man, an actual person, one of whom you had no prior notice or regard—the very idea! How dare you allow strange men to take you up in their carriages?" demanded her ladyship.

"I tell you it was perfectly all right. I had a short conversation with his mother—"

"But if he is a duke then his mother must have been a duchess!"

"Precisely! The Dowager Duchess of Pevensey."

There was a look of exasperation in Lady Pollworth's eyes as she stared at her daughter. Finally, she said in a sarcastic tone: "And, of course, she was also entertaining Her Royal Highness. I am sure you all must have had a most delightful tea."

Pamela laughed. "You do not believe me, do you?"

"Of course, I do not. How can I, Pamela? You come into me with a Banbury tale that no one in his right mind would credit. Now, be a dear child and tell me what occurred. In truth, now!"

"Mama, it is quite as I say. It *was* the Duke of Pevensey that I chatted with, and it *was* his mother, the duchess, whom he took me in to meet. It was no great thing. After a while he carried me home and here I am to tell the tale."

"And a pretty tale it is! You say this duke was a young man?"

"Yes, and his name is Gerald. They live just over in Bloomsbury Square."

"How very enlightening! And I presume that he will have a wish to meet with your parents?"

"He did not put it quite that way, Mama, but he did say that he would like to get acquainted—with Geoffrey, too."

"Oh dear, oh dear! Pamela, I do not know what I shall do with you. I just cannot take what you are telling me all that seriously. As if I did not have enough to do, now I have got to worry about entertaining dukes and duchesses. Good heavens, girl, what am I to do? Shall I call upon her Grace?"

"I could not truly say. It was all so informal, you see. I just went up to the door and knocked—Oh!" she exclaimed suddenly, realizing that she was beginning to give the story away.

"Aha!" cried Lady Pollworth. "There is something more, is there? You never mentioned that it was you who called upon them!"

Pamela's face crimsoned. "I dare say I did not," she offered lamely.

"Daughter, may I inquire as to precisely what it was that took you to the door of the Duke of Pevensey? At this point, it is safe to say that you had an ulterior motive, would you agree?"

"Oh, Mama, it was just that I did not think that you would speak to Papa, and I hoped to get a chance to speak to his Grace's chef, you see. For goodness sake, there was a perfectly good chef going begging. Until we can get Papa to make up his mind, I did not think that it would be wrong to go and speak with the fellow."

"So it was, that out of a clear blue sky, you decided to go blithely up to the Duke of Pevensey's door and demand to see his disaffected chef. Really, Pamela, that is not at all the thing!"

Pamela could not think of a thing to say at that instant.

"Do you say it was not?" asked her mother.

"The way it turned out, fortunately it was not. That is, I never did get an opportunity to speak with the fellow—but I did ascertain his name. It is Hippolyte Galliard."

"I shall thank you for that information when I can comprehend its worth—But I do not see how it could not have been embarrassing for you. If someone came to inquire whether Mrs. Biggam's services were available, I should be highly incensed. Indeed I should."

"Yes, yes. I realize that now, but nothing came of it because I met the duke before anything was said—practically."

"What was said?" demanded her mother, quickly.

"Not a word to his Grace I assure you. It was just that I inquired of his footman about the chef. Then, before anything could be done about it, he happened along, and I thought it wiser to let the matter drop."

"I certainly should hope so! Did he not take exception to the fact that you had come unescorted to call upon him?"

"The duchess did pass a remark—"

"We are ruined!" cried Lady Pollworth.

"Not at all! Everything was most cordial, and I am

sure that we shall be hearing from their Graces before too long."

"Do you truly think so, my dear?" asked her ladyship, blinking her eyes rapidly in interest.

"I shall be something surprised if we do not, and more than a little disappointed. His Grace is such a very charming gentleman."

"I am so pleased to hear it. One can always do with charming neighbors. So it is in Bloomsbury Square that they dwell. My, how very convenient!"

Pamela laughed gleefully. "That is precisely what his Grace remarked, Mama. How very convenient!"

The Duke of Pevensey was still smiling as he drove onto the grounds of the Foundling Hospital; but the sight that greeted him at the front door of the institution quickly wiped it away. Two very disreputable characters were standing, or rather struggling with each other, in the drive, and he could easily recognize what was left of his footman and his new tiger.

Twemlow's livery was all covered with mud and there were gaping rents about his padded shoulders. His silk stockings were utter ruins and his buckled slippers were unspeakable.

As for Bertie, patches of his red coat were discernible beneath the mud and grass stains, his little knees were peeking out of two similar windows, gaping wide, and were as filthy as all the rest of him.

His Grace's humor was not of the best as he dismounted from his curricle and demanded: "Twemlow, I am deeply disappointed in you! Can you not keep proper charge of a small child?"

"With all due respect, your Grace, I am sure that I can, but this is never a child but a fiend in a child's form. No sooner than you were passed out of the gate,

91

he announced his intention of going off to the navy. He would prefer being a cabin boy to being your tiger—"

"Fiddlesticks! It is just the talk of a small boy."

"So I thought, your Grace, except for the fact that he immediately made a dash for the highway. You would be surprised how fast those little legs can go! Thank heaven, I was on the alert for anything and quickly caught up with him. But, no, that was not enough. Like an eel, I tell you, he slipped from my grasp and made a dash to the rear of the grounds. This time, only the necessity of having to negotiate the wall held him up sufficiently for me to get my hands on him. Unfortunately, in the process I fell, and there was a further struggle in the loam—as you can see, your Grace. I am exceedingly distressed and embarrassed, your Grace, and I must protest this duty you have put me to. If it is to continue, I deeply regret that I shall have no recourse but to give notice."

"All right, Twemlow, I shall keep that in mind. Now I would hear what our dear Bertie has to say for himself. Well, young man, I am waiting. I thought that you preferred my service to remaining in the hospital. If you do not, I must find me another, more appreciative boy, to serve me as tiger."

Bertie began to sniffle.

"None of that! I want no cry-babies in my service. I am a duke and must have only the bravest and the best."

Bertie frowned and looked up earnestly at his Grace.

"What abaht th' lydy?" he asked, and there was a challenging note in his voice.

"The lady? Miss Pollworth? What about the lady?"

"What 've ye done wi' 'er?"

"I merely carried her to her home in Mecklenburg Square, which is just across the square from this place."

"Ah, then Oi'll go ter be *her* tiger, that's what! Oi likes her, Oi does!"

"There is no call for you to get huffy about it. The lady has not any need of a tiger. In fact, ladies do not have tigers. They have pages, instead."

"Right you are, guv'nor; Oi'll be her pyge, I will!"

The duke regarded him for a moment with a sigh. "Methinks you are incorrigible, my little man. I am not your governor; I am your Grace—and, for all I know, Miss Pollworth may have a page. In any case, I am sure that you are not cut out for the post. For one thing, you are not black, and for another, you are not any one's idea of a lady's companion. Now, I caution you to put all of this nonsense out of your mind. You shall be my tiger or you shall not.

"I have signed all the necessary papers, and it is in my power to make you do what I say; but I do not wish it to be so. Do you wish to be my tiger or no?"

For a moment, Bertie gave the matter his most solemn consideration. He looked up at Twemlow's great height and inquired: "Does they all be like he, yer Gryce?"

"No, he is the tallest of all my servants. It is naught for you to worry about. I shall put you in charge of my butler, Plunkett, who is shorter than myself—if that is what is worrying you."

"Aye, it wore, yer Gryce. But s'pose Oi ain't happy in it?"

"If it should turn out that way, I shall have you brought back to the hospital."

Bertie's expression turned sour. "I dessay Oi'll like it, right enough."

"Excellent. Then, if you are satisfied, I pray that we may leave for home."

* * *

But unfortunately for the duke's peace of mind, all matters had not been settled. Twemlow suggested that the boy ride up behind and he sit with the duke within the carriage.

"I had another idea," rejoined his Grace. "We shall all sit together inside the curricle. The boy is not up to riding behind. He shall have to be taught."

"Then, if it is all the same to you, your Grace, I shall ride behind. The little beast is filthy—"

"You are in no better case, and I am not about to have the world see me driving about with a footman who has all the appearance of having been in a smash-up.

"Enough of this nonsense! Twemlow, get into the curricle and take the boy on your lap. I tell you it will be all right. The both of you are in need of baths, and I dare say I shall be in need of one after this business is done with as well!"

The iron note of anger in his tone brought about instant compliance. Without further ado, they all got into the carriage and the duke drove it away.

Chapter VII

To say the least, the short drive back to Pevensey House was unpleasant. Bertie was not comfortable on Twemlow's lap, and he stated his case loudly and frequently. Twemlow, mindful of the duke's temper, fumed silently, while he attempted to quell the outbursts of the little fiend on his lap. His Grace concentrated his efforts upon the traffic in the streets, preferring not to think about the nuisance he was about to saddle his domicile with. He was no longer so sanguine about his choice of tiger and, had it not been for the recollection of Miss Pollworth's plea in the latter's behalf, he might well have turned the curricle about and deposited the imp back at the Foundling Hospital.

By the time they had pulled up in front of the ducal residence in Bloomsbury Square, Bertie had shut up and was now sitting with a sullen look upon his face.

He appeared to have exhausted himself in complaint, and every now and again, glanced quizzically at his new master.

His Grace dismounted from the carriage and handed over the reins and Master Bertie to the groom who came out to the carriage, with instructions for Bertie's future care, maintenance and education. When the groom understood that all of this instruction was not for himself but was to be relayed to the head coachman, he looked mightily relieved. Taking Bertie's grimy hand in his, he marched him alongside as he led the carriage horses back to the mews behind the great house.

Twemlow already had his hand on the front door handle when his Grace called him back. With the look of a man who was proceeding to his execution, Twemlow came forward.

"Your Grace, if there was anything I said that your Grace took exception to, I offer my humble apology—"

"No, no, Twemlow, it is quite all right. I understand perfectly the burden I placed upon you. Bertie is something more than a handful, and I venture to say that life at Pevensey House, for all of us, is about to undergo a transformation that we may all regret. No, put it out of your mind. I have something else I would discuss with you."

"Your Grace is both kind and considerate," said Twemlow, very much relieved.

"I suspect that Bertie might take vehement issue with you upon that score—but never mind. I would ask you about Miss Pollworth. Since you appeared to have been in search of me, if you will recall, and since I have not been able to ascertain Miss Pollworth's reasons for calling upon me, I thought that you might know something of the circumstances that led to the lady's appearance in the hall of Pevensey House."

"Ah, as to that, your Grace, I was the person who responded to Miss Pollworth's knock, and I can assure your Grace that it was not you whom she inquired for."

"But that is odd. She did not seem overly interested to meet with her Grace, either."

"Oh, but, your Grace, it was Galliard the lady asked for. I thought it somewhat irregular that she should have done so, and went in search of your Grace."

"Galliard? Now that is a strange thing," mused the duke. Then, he said: "Very well, Twemlow, that will be all. Get yourself cleaned up; but, before you do, alert my valet to the state of my person. I shall be needing a complete change of apparel. Just see what that little devil has done to my pantaloons with his muddy boots!"

The butler greeted his Grace as he came through the door, with a look of great consternation. He was actually wringing his hands in despair.

"Oh, your Grace, I do not know what to tell you. I have spoken to her Grace, but she has refused to take any part in it, and has referred me to you, your Grace. I am sure I do not know what to do!"

"Heavens, man, you are wailing about like some forsaken spirit! Nothing can be as bad as all that, especially as I have had a very poor day thus far. Spit it out! Where's the trouble? Surely, it cannot be Bertie! There has not been time!"

Plunkett stared in astonishment at his master. "Bertie, your Grace? We have no Bertie, to my knowledge. No, it is Galliard, your Grace. He is acting like a red savage on the warpath. Something is out with him, but he will not say what it is. He demands to

97

have a word with you, your Grace; only you! Oh dear!" he cried, in despair, as through one of the doors to the entrance hall, a large man came marching, brandishing a huge wooden spoon as though it were a baton of rank. On his head he wore a chef's high bonnet, black to match the color of the soot which was always showering down out of the great hoods of his coal-fired cooking grates, and his corpulent figure was swathed in a great white apron which plainly showed the marks of his profession.

The pudginess of his countenance was somewhat hidden by a large black mustache which usually drooped down at both ends of his lips, but now they showed a tendency to curl, so great was the man's agitation.

"Excellency! Excellency! To Hippolyte you have given ze blessure fatale! Regardez, monseigneur! All over Hippolyte is le sang de mon coeur!"

"The good Lord give me strength!" murmured the duke. To his chef, he snapped: "Fiddlesticks! There is nothing but sauce all over your filthy apron, man! What in blazes do you want now!"

"Ah, monseigneur, you are cold! So cold! Monseigneur, as cold as ze ice is your heart!"

"Perhaps I have need of a doctor of medicine. Galliard, state the nonsense that is bothering you and let me get to my chambers! As you can see, I am not in fit condition to stand about in conversation with anyone, least of all you. Don't you ever change your apron?"

The chef shrugged and said in a mild tone: "To what purpose, monseigneur? In seconds, it would be decoloré—"

"Discolored? Bah! Filthy is the word! Galliard, do you have something to say? If not, I have something to say to you!"

"Hein? À moi, monseigneur?" His eyes lit up. "Ah, zen you know! And to Hippolyte you have come to make ze grande excuse!"

"Devil take you, what are you driving at? No, of course, I am not about to apologize to you! What is on your liver, anyway?"

The light in Galliard's eyes quickly died, to be replaced by a mournful look. "Ah, zen you are dissatisfy wiz Hippolyte! I go, monseigneur, nevair to return!"

For all the resignation in his voice, the chef made no move to depart.

The Duke stared at him. "Pray tell me, chef of mine, are you mad or is it that you are French?"

The chef sadly shook his head and shook his wooden spoon at the same time. "Tsk! Tsk! I see ze monseigneur would jest. Ah me, it is time for Hippolyte to go to la France! It is—"

"Plunkett, what ails this Gallic horror?" demanded his Grace.

Plunkett begged to be excused.

"No, dammit! You stay and help me with this imbecile. Now, Galliard, I am fast losing patience with you. By God, if you continue to sputter at me, I shall—"

"Ze collation, monseigneur! It is ze collation. You did not like, monseigneur, and ze heart of Hippolyte is broke!"

This dramatic statement called for an equally dramatic gesture. In bringing his hand to his breast, Galliard forgot the spoon it was holding, and managed to deliver himself a rap on the side of his large nose that brought tears to his eyes. While he stood there blinking in pain for a moment, the duke chuckled, and Plunkett hid a smile with his hand.

Waxing more indignant than ever, the chef now did make a move to leave.

"Steady on, Galliard! Let us get to the bottom of this, once and for all!" cried the duke. "What collation are you talking about? I have no recollection of any collation."

Much aggrieved, the chef replied: "It was ze collation I 'ave assemblé for ze guest of monseigneur, Mademoiselle Pollworth."

"Oh, *that* collation! Why, I never tasted the blasted thing!"

"Eggzackly, monsieur le duc! You did not like!"

"I do not know if I liked it or not, you idiot! How could I, if I did not taste it?"

"But how could you not? It was of ze mos' *délectable*, monseigneur! Zey tell me le monseigneur is entertain' a lady of la plus belle, so I 'ave assemblé ze finest mets à la cuisine! Caviar, ze finest! Pâté de foie gras au truffes! Galantine de capon! *Oeufs en gelée*! Zen for sweet *tarte aux fraises*! And for to drink, *la belle champagne* an', because ze mamselle she is anglaise—ugh!——ratafia! C'est une collation de plus délectable!

"Monseigneur, for you I give all, but what do I get for zis? Rien! You do not even taste! La mademoiselle, non! La duchesse, non! Le duc, non! Je suis désolé!"

His Grace was not very disturbed by the tirade. He said: "Yes, it sounds a perfectly marvelous spread. I pray that there is something left of it, for I could eat a bear!"

Immediately, Galliard's features were alight. "Ah, monseigneur, très bon! I go to make ready, toute de suite!"

"All in good time, my irascible Gaul! First, I wish to know—where did you meet Miss Pollworth? How did you come to know her?"

"Moi, monseigneur? Nevair! Nevair 'ave I see this ladee! What for you ask zis of me?"

"It is my understanding that Miss Pollworth inquired for you, when she called."

"Oho!" cried the chef, his eyes opening wide and his lips matching it in a grin that quite split the roundness of his face. Even his mustache seemed to stiffen with joy at the news. "So! À la fin, Hippolyte becomes known to ze anglaises!"

"You miserable French gossoon, cease preening yourself! Then, it is clear that you had no knowledge of Miss Pollworth before this. Is that a fact?"

"Oui, Monseigneur. I do not know zis ladee, but I should be enchanté to mak' ze acquaintance wiz zis ladee!"

"I strongly suspect that she would not welcome the encounter. Very well, Hippolyte, you may return to your kitchen—and the next time, do you make it plain to Plunkett what your business with me is. It is not at all fitting for the cook to buttonhole the master at any time he pleases—"

"Monseigneur, I beg ze *pardon*! I am nevair ze cook! Here I am ze *chef*! In ze cuisine, zere is no one above Hippolyte Galliard! As for Monsieur Plunkett, pfah! He I do not care for. Of ze cuisine, he knows nothing. Eh bien, Monseigneur, I kiss your hand. For ze Mademoiselle Pollworth, I give to you ze congratulation if she is to be ze new duchesse!"

"Away with you, incorrigible impertinent!" said the duke laughing. He turned to Plunkett. "I dare say you are not our maestro's favorite. At the risk of augmenting his animosity towards you, I must insist that you keep him in his kitchen in the future, even if you have to shackle him to his blasted ovens!"

* * *

Still, his Grace had not heard the last of Hippolyte Galliard. The next time it was a complaint from his mother, the duchess. After he had, with the assistance of his valet refreshed himself and donned a change of apparel, he was informed by Plunkett that her Grace had a wish to speak with him. Being a more or less dutiful son, he attended upon his mother in her sitting room.

"Where are on earth have you been, Gerald? I have had a wish to speak with you concerning our cook. He has got to be told to be less extravagant, less French in his ideas of what to serve. That collation, for instance, we had with Miss Pollworth. It was a disgrace! One would have thought that there was a wedding party in the vicinity. It was too—too flamboyant by far, to serve a neighbor's little girl.

"By the way, your Grace, I never did get to understand the reason for that young person's calling upon me. Is there some sort of mystery in it, or is she something of a climber?"

"A climber? No, I do not think so. As a matter of fact, I thought—"

"At the moment, your Grace, I would much prefer to settle with this cook of yours. Caviar and champagne in the midst of the day! The very idea. Now that young lady will be spreading it all about the neighborhood how extravagant we are. Gerald, you have just got to do something about that cook!"

"It was all well intentioned. Hippolyte was of the opinion that I had some special interest in Miss Pollworth and was going to the greatest length, you see. But I shall speak to the fellow. I dare say I would have before this, but I have other things on my mind at the moment."

"Ah, the ever so charming Miss Pollworth," rejoined

her Grace, drily, although there was a touch of curiosity in her tone.

The duke chuckled. "Really, my dear, you sound a typical mother! It is hardly the lady, I do assure you. As a matter of fact, I have engaged me a tiger—a little lad who promises to make me a greater problem than he is worth. I dropped by the Foundling Hospital and found him there."

"Hmm. Most commendable in you, Gerald; but, if you do not mind, I shall reserve my opinion in this instance. She was quite adorable, I do admit, and I could not help but notice she did not sample a bite—not that I could blame her for that! However, my dear son, the fact that you did not appear to have any appetite for Galliard's lavish spread spoke volumes to me."

His Grace merely shrugged. "Have it as you will, ma mère. I know that nothing I say to the contrary will change your opinion. I admit that I was not aware of the food and that, for the simple reason that my mind was engaged in trying to determine precisely why the lady had come to call upon us all by herself. You will be interested to learn that, actually, it was neither for you nor for me that she inquired, but for Hippolyte."

The duchess stared at her son in amazement. "She came to call upon our cook? Oh, Gerald, I pray that there is no scandal in this. You must sack that beastly Frenchman at once! I will not tolerate such behavior! And that female! Why—"

"Your Grace, I bid you not to say a word more!" snapped the duke angrily. "I do not know what this is all about, yet; but I have every intention of discovering what is behind it. Until then, I prefer not to speculate upon it, nor listen to your remarks. We, neither of us, have a right to any opinion on the matter."

"That may serve *you*, my son, but it does not serve me! Until I hear something to the girl's favor, I have no wish to receive her, or *any* of the Pollworths."

"That does not suit me, for I intend to investigate the business and I cannot do that if I put the Pollworths beneath my notice. You have your choice, your Grace, of continuing as my hostess, or betaking you down to Pevensey where you will not be bothered by the Pollworths. They shall be amongst my guests at my very next function."

The duchess frowned. "That is a hard choice, your Grace; but I see a mother's duty to her idiot son. At whatever cost to my pride, and the dignity of the Lyttons, I shall stay on. If you are about to make a cake of yourself over a loose-skirt, I want to be there!"

The duke let out a sharp bark of laughter. "I never doubted that you would desert me in this awful time of stress, mother of mine!"

Chapter VIII

Unlike the other squares in Bloomsbury that had been inhabited for a while, Mecklenburg was only in the process of being settled. There were still vacant plots and vacant houses. Although they were all in the process of becoming occupied, there was a newness to the little neighborhood that contributed a spirit of informality, not to be experienced in well-settled, high-class, London dwelling spaces.

As a result, Lady Pollworth, by the time she was satisfied that her plans for her first affair in the new house were acceptable, had become very well acquainted with her neighbors. Nonetheless, she was loath to commence the social activities of the Pollworths until the formal rituals of calling and receiving had been accomplished. As the weather continued quite severe, the process was a long time in completing.

Winter's gelid grip was showing the first signs of

infirmity when, to her great surprise, invitations to different affairs in the neighborhood began to appear on the little writing table upon which she accomplished all her holographic efforts.

It not only caught her by surprise, but it also threw her into such a depth of confusion, she was forced to consult with Lord Pollworth. But, since that worthy gentleman was totally concerned with Napoleon's misadventures, he asked her not to bother him with inconsequentialities, and to use her own good judgment in the matter. It was a high compliment indeed, for Lord Pollworth had rarely if ever trusted his lady's judgment before.

The business was beyond Lady Pollworth's estimate of her own capability, and so she now turned to Pamela for assistance in making up her mind.

Pamela took advantage of her mother's indecision to delay matters. She cautioned against any rash action, hoping to postpone the opening of Pollworth House to Society until she had been able to solve the dilemma of the Pollworth table.

Some weeks had passed since she had made the attempt to gain access to the Pevensey chef, and that failure had quite discouraged her from making another. She had hoped that the Duke of Pevensey, as a good neighbor might, would have invited the Pollworths to Pevensey House. That would have made it easy for her to pursue the undertaking. But days had passed without any word from his direction, and she was sure that another way, perhaps even another chef, would have to be discovered.

In the meantime, she put all her efforts into blocking her mother's plans. As the day came nearer when they would have to begin to indicate their acceptance of the various invitations, Lady Pollworth began to wilt under the pressure of the impending decisions. She was quickly achieving a state of mind which boded no good for Pamela's hopes, and Pamela was now exhausted in her excuses to defer the Pollworth's own affair.

Things had come to such a pass Lady Pollworth was commencing the laborious efforts of composing the model of the invitation that she felt obliged to send out. The reason for her extensive labors was due entirely to the fact that, once again, in these exertions of composition, she was influenced by every new invitation that arrived. She was sure that the latest was far more fitting and proper than any she had received previously, and of course, her own invitations had to reflect the "best" as she understood it. The delay these revisions caused were a blessing to Pamela.

The mail, one morning, brought an invitation that quite wiped away all of Pamela's objections. It was from the Dowager Duchess of Pevensey announcing a ball. It was expressly stated that the affair was for the purpose of bringing together those illustrious families newly arrived in the Bloomsbury district with those who had preceded them. It was, upon the face of it, a most hospitable gesture and raised great anticipations in the breasts of Pamela and her mother.

It also reduced Lady Pollworth's plans to complete confusion, and exacerbated the turmoil in her ladyship's bosom. Although it was difficult to make much complaint about the duchess's cordiality, she did manage a few remarks before she allowed herself to be overwhelmed by the prospect and joined her daughter in a period of rejoicing. It became apparent to her that after all the formal introductions had been accomplished at the Pevensey affair, she would be able to invite any one she pleased, and without having to stand upon ceremony. That in itself was a great relief and much to be desired.

Pamela saw it as a means of delaying her mother's plans for a long time, and also of allowing her an opportunity to try once again to interview Monsieur Hippolyte Galliard. Now that this hope was renewed, she suffered from a certain anxiety. She recalled that, although the duke and his chef appeared to be at odds, his Grace was amused rather than annoyed by the fellow and so she was not optimistic about her chances of intruding upon that odd association. Furthermore, she had not the slightest idea of the amount of wages a French chef demanded, but she was sure that the wages of a Mrs. Biggam must be miniscule by comparison.

Still, things were now much more favorable. Once again, a visitor to Pevensey House, together with a host of other guests, she was bound to find a way to speak with the fellow, even if it meant deserting the party for a short sojourn belowstairs. In the confusion of a large affair, her absence for a little time would never be noticed.

That so great a lady would condescend to sponsor a gathering limited to her friends and neighbors in Bloomsbury was quite remarkable, and it called for lengthy conversations amongst the recipients of the invitations. First, of course, it was necessary to determine who, if any one, had been neglected. Then the significance of the event had to be thoroughly debated. Finally, after the inhabitants of Mecklenburg Square had assured themselves that the duchess had included all of the nobility, and that the affair was nothing more or less than a demonstration of neighborliness, they got down to the serious business of deciding on the apparel they would don for this momentous occasion.

All of this was true for the matrons of the neighborhood, and it was even more so, if that were possible, for their eligible daughters. The younger set managed to have their own cozes upon the topic, meeting daily at a different house about the square.

For a while, Pamela had very little to contribute to the discussions. It was only as she listened, that she came to understand how influential were the Pevenseys in the social world, particularly the Dowager. She was so pleased that she had not revealed her true reason for having made the call, that she could have hugged herself. It was obvious to her that Twemlow had not said a word in that regard, or her family would have never received an invitation. The thought must have been mirrored upon her face.

Miss Fairchild cast a quizzical glance at her and asked: "Whatever are you so pleased about, Pamela? You have the look of Puss with a fresh-caught fish before her."

Replied Pamela, offhandedly: "I was just thinking how pleasant it would be to renew my acquaintanceship with their Graces."

"Their Graces?" echoed Miss Blandish. "Have you known the Lyttons from before?"

"No. It was but recently that I met with the duke and the duchess," she replied, wondering at the way her friends were all staring at her.

Henrietta Blandish turned to the others and said, sarcastically: "Can you imagine that? She has met with the duke and duchess but recently."

Quickly she turned back to Pamela and cried: "For heaven's sake, Pamela, you cannot stop there! Did you call upon them or did they call upon you? How did it come about? What of the duke? Is he as charming as I have heard tell?"

It had been a cozy little group before, but now, as the girls all clustered closer to Pamela, it was even cozier. They were all staring at her, hardly daring to breathe lest they miss a word of what was to follow.

"I assure you it was nothing so very special as all that," said Pamela defensively. "We—er just happened to meet and they were very pleasant to me. We sat down together for a collation, talked a bit, and then his Grace was kind enough to drive me home."

The little group exploded into shrieks of delight. "You were actually in his carriage with him?" "Where were your parents?" "Pray how did it all come about?" "Oh, how I envy you!" "Pamela, tell us more!"

Pamela was quite taken aback at the furor she had raised. For the moment, she was not sure of what she ought to say. She was certain that she did not wish to reveal to her friends any part of the reason for having gone to Pevensey House. The less said about that aspect, the better. Yet, she had to say something. She offered up a silent prayer that none of her friends would recall her interest in securing a chef, and went on to explain: "It was such a little business. I thought to take a stroll about the neighborhood, and when I came into Bloomsbury Square, I was taken with one of the great houses there. I am sure you will agree that there was nothing exceptional to my going up to the door to inquire as to the identity of the proprietor—"

"Oh, Pamela, but you were all alone! Oh, how very daring it was of you!" exclaimed Miss Margery Dawling. "I should never have had the audacity!"

"I am sure that none of us would, my dear," said Henrietta. "It is inconceivable that any of us would have had the poor taste to go unescorted beyond the limits of Mecklenburg Square."

"Oh, hush you, Henrietta!" exclaimed Eleanor. "I am sure that you would have gone a deal farther if it meant meeting with his Grace. Pamela, disregard Henrietta and tell us what happened next."

Henrietta gave a toss of her head and settled back, as anxious as any of the others to hear Pamela's tale.

"A footman responded, but I venture to say that he misunderstood the purpose of my inquiry and went off to fetch his master." She stopped there, paused to study the rapt faces of her audience, and then went on to say: "The duke happened to be passing. He was very pleasant and we went in to meet the duchess, his mother. That was all there was to it."

Pamela's mind was racing to imagine what questions would now be thrown at her, still very fearful that Henrietta or Eleanor might recall the reference to his Grace's chef during a previous conversation. Her fears were realized.

Eleanor asked: "Did you have a chance to sample any food prepared by the duke's chef?"

That was not so bad, thought Pamela as she replied: "A cold collation was served, but as neither her Grace nor the duke partook, I did not think it fitting."

"Ah, that was not lucky, my dear. I am sure it would have been a treat. By the way, has your father found himself a proper chef as yet?"

Pamela shook her head and then carried the conversation into a tale of how preoccupied Lord Pollworth was with the nasty war. At once, each of the ladies discovered she had a similar tale to tell, and Pamela's little ordeal was over, at least as far as the question of a chef was concerned. None of the ladies had been at all satisfied with the paucity of details that she had recited concerning the handsome, young Duke of Pevensey, so that, before the visit was concluded, she was forced to give her impressions of the young man. Of course, they were pleasant ones.

This brought the conversation about to the Lady Charlotte, the ladies being particularly intent upon discovering how the duchess carried herself. Pamela was not about to admit that she had found the duchess formidable, but it did not matter. Her friends were sure that the Dowager was quite the most puissant lady in the district, and gave full vent to their apprehensions about their deportment when they came to meet the powerful peeress.

During her short walk back to her house, Pamela's mind was quite busy. She was aware that her friends believed that she had ingratiated herself with the Duchess of Pevensey and that she had a special status with the duke. By the time the visit broke up, she realized that, as none of the others had ever met the Lyttons, much less been inside their house, she had been accorded an unspoken social superiority. At the party, she would have already gained the notice that each of them devoutly wished for. The speculation that followed was only natural, and it had to do with the question of whom the duke would ask to partner him in the various dances.

None of the ladies expected there was any chance they would be singled out for one of the early dances. As the ranking nobleman, the Duke would be expected to do the proper with a number of higher ranking ladies before he would be free to dance with some one of his own choice. As there were bound to be more eligible young ladies present than he could possibly dance with, only a few fortunate ones would be so honored. Obviously, Pamela had a better chance than most in that regard, so that the final parting was one not unmixed with envy for the fact that she was already in his Grace's acquaintance.

Pamela had nothing to say to her mother about the thoughts that the visit with her friends had given rise to, but Lady Pollworth had something to say to her as a result of her own conversations with the neighbors.

It was after dinner, and Lord Pollworth had excused himself to go to his library, where he had some papers that required his attention. Lady Pollworth made no objection, but she did frown discontentedly, once he was gone out of the room.

"Oh, Pamela, your father worries me so!" she exclaimed. "I would not be at all surprised if he were unable to attend the Pevensey affair. You know how it has been of late. He is forever on pins and needles, lest Bonaparte steal a march on him. I do not understand how whatever Bonaparte decides to do can affect us, but your father insists it is so, and so I must believe him. But I never shall understand him. I do declare, if we must miss out on the Pevensey party, I shall never forgive Bonaparte!" she ended angrily.

"Mama, it will not come to that, I am sure. Papa must attend, we all must, or give affront to the Lyttons."

"I find it rather odd," began Lady Pollworth, going off on another tack, "that none of the families on our square have gained the notice of the duke and duchess before this. Of course, it is not to be wondered at. Bloomsbury Square is not in our immediate vicinity, and the nobility who reside there are at the top of the stairs. Two dukes, mind you—"

"Just the one, Mama. The Duke of Bedford did have
113

his house there, but it was razed many years ago to make room for all the new developments."

"Oh, can it be so? I was sure that his Grace was still connected with the neighborhood—"

"He is, but as a landlord. I understand that practically all of Bloomsbury is in his holding."

"In that case, it is almost the same. As I was saying, they are very high in the instep there, in Bloomsbury Square, and have a right to be, what with two dukes. But now I wonder. Does the Duke of Pevensey pay his rent to the Duke of Bedford? If that be so, then I should think that the Duke of Pevensey is not a very wealthy duke."

Pamela laughed. "Of course he is. You should see the table that he spreads for just a light nuncheon—and the lavish decoration of the rooms! Mama, I do not know which of them is the wealthier, but I am sure that there is not much to choose between them."

"Which brings me to a point concerning which I have had a mind to discuss with you, Daughter. I still am not at all clear how it came about that, of all the young ladies who reside in Mecklenburg Square, you, and you alone, are the only one to have made the acquaintance of the Lyttons. They can hardly be so formidable as is thought, if you had but to knock upon their door to get to know them."

Pamela began to feel uncomfortable. "Oh, Mama, must we go all over that business again? They are people just like every one else—and it just happened. His Grace is, perhaps, a year or two older than Geoffrey, and as pleasant, if not pleasanter. Why, do you know that on the way back to Mecklenburg Square, we stopped off at the Foundling Hospital so that his Grace could find himself a tiger—"

"A tiger?!" Lady Pollworth let out a little shriek.

"You may be calm, Mama. It is not a beast, I have reference to; it is merely a small boy who is engaged by a gentleman to look after his horses. He is something of a groom, and something of a footman, to serve the small carriages that gentlemen of fashion are given to driving. I am sure you have seen the sort I mean."

"Ah, yes, I have seen them, hanging on behind—but I had thought they were pages. Why on earth should they be called tigers?"

"I haven't the slightest notion."

Lady Pollworth shook her head in disapproval. "I should hope that your father has better sense. A nice, large footman, makes a deal more sense. Of what use a little chap if one is beset by highwaymen and footpads?"

"It is just that these sporting curricles are too tiny to give a footman an easy hold. I know this, for Twemlow was having the greatest difficulty—"

"Twemlow? Who is Twemlow?"

Said Pamela: "Oh, I am sure I informed you. He is the duke's footman."

Lady Pollworth fluttered her eyes at her daughter. "Pamela, this all comes as news to me. I am beginning to think that you have not told me a thing about your visit to the Duke of Pevensey. You are acquainted with the duke's footman. You have gone with him to the Foundling Hospital to assist him in procuring a servant of some sort. I demand to know exactly how long this business with the duke has been going on. I suspect that the Duke of Pevensey is less than a gentleman, and he is taking advantage of you. Suddenly, everything is very suspicious. I am even beginning to suspect that the invitation we have received has been tendered in a most questionable light."

"Oh, Mama, no!" exclaimed Pamela in dismay. "It

was only that one time, I tell you. There was nothing exceptional in it. His Grace was a perfect gentleman. If you knew the duchess, you would know he had to be. She is not the sort of lady to stand for any nonsense."

"You cannot know how much it relieves me to hear you say so," responded her mother drily. "Still, it is but a dowager duchess and he is a duke. Pamela, you talk as if you had known her Grace for the better part of a lifetime. If it was but the one visit, I do not see how you can have gained such a great knowledge of the Lyttons in so little time. I am sure you will embarrass me before all my friends. Pamela, this must not continue. If his Grace is the gentleman you claim, then he must come to meet your father, do you hear?"

"Mama, how can I assure you that it is nothing so serious. Why, it is I, who would be embarrassed, to even suggest it to him. It was naught but a pleasant little time we spent together, nothing more. Oh, Mama, I do wish you would put the entire business out of your mind. Now, if we alone had received an invitation to the Pevensey's affair, there might have been something in it, but it happens not to be the case. I suspect that it is just their way of getting to know all the new people, like ourselves, who have moved into Bloomsbury in recent months. Why, do you know that her Grace does not even believe Mecklenburg Square is a part of Bloomsbury?"

"Now, there you go again, Pamela. How can you possibly know what her Grace believes, if you have not been in many conversations with her. I tell you something is there, my child, and you are too young to know what you are doing!"

A note of hysteria was coloring Lady Pollworth's voice.

She had not finished and went on to say: "I think I must take this matter up with your father. He shall have to have a talk with that young man, duke or no."

The threat quite routed Pamela. To save every one from the embarrassment that must arise if her father were to speak to his Grace, it was now necessary to convince her mother that matters were never so serious as she believed.

"Mama, you are making much, too much, of it!" she cried. "I tell you it was only the one time. Actually, I should not have met the duke at all but for that horrid footman!"

"Child, what are you saying? A horrid footman? Who has a horrid footman? His Grace?"

There was a look of pain on Pamela's face as she said, in an agony of resignation: "Mama, I did not tell you the entire truth of the matter. It was all because of the chef. I assure you, if only Papa had agreed to it, nothing like this would have occurred. I went into Bloomsbury Square that day, because I had heard that his Grace and his chef did not get along. You see, I thought that we might get him for ourselves—"

"Pamela Pollworth, how could you have done such an outrageous thing! I was right, all along. I told your father that London was not anyplace to bring up a daughter in a proper fashion, but would he heed me? No, not at all!

"A chef, mind you! A chef, and never a duke! Oh, what shame! I shall never be able to show my face again!"

But Pamela was practiced in the art of restoring her mother to a semblance of reason, and it took her only a matter of twenty minutes, together with an application, or two, of spirits of hartshorn, to enable her mother to recover sufficiently so that the entire story of that day's events could be laid before her.

The detailing of her adventure, proved to be an ardous task, for the reason that her mother had been a country gentlewoman all her life, and had grave reservations about London Society, and all the nuances which she did not understand. But she was ever fearful of being singled out as unworldly. As a result, she went to the trouble of examining each and every incident that Pamela could recall, trying to determine if there were anything to take exception to.

The deeper into the recitation that Pamela traveled, the greater was Lady Pollworth's disappointment, and it was mirrored upon her countenance. She could not, for the life of her, see anything either exceptional, or encouraging in what her daughter was telling her.

By the time Pamela had finished explaining that his Grace had expressed his willingness to call upon her ladyship but that his costume of that time had not been sufficiently presentable to allow it, Lady Pollworth's disappointment was complete.

She said, in an irritated manner: "I truly do not see that there is anything to be made of it. Actually, his Grace's manner was quite correct, under the circumstance. It was you, Pamela, who was most decidedly at fault.

"Truly, it is a shame. Everyone to whom I mentioned the fact that you were personally acquainted with the Duke of Pevensey made so much of it. Ah well, young lady, let it be a lesson to you. You are never to go out so far from home again without someone with you. You have got your maid and there are our own footmen—and I should hope that they know how to treat a gentlewoman more fittingly than that Twemlow

118

of his Grace's—But, Pamela, you have got to promise to be more circumspect in your behavior. This is London, you know. It is a far cry from Surrey. They do things differently in the city, and we have got to follow suit if we do not wish to have fingers pointed at us. I know I do not wish for that."

"Yes, Mama—"

"But, of course, I shall have to speak to your father about Mrs. Biggam. She just will not do, you know. I have gathered, these past few days, that a French chef in the kitchen—well, one just cannot be without one if one expects to be noticed in polite Society. I understand that even merchants have Frenchmen for chefs—and valets, too! Can you imagine that? And there is your father, very satisfied to have not a single Frenchman about the premises. We are quite out of fashion, I fear. Yes, I shall have to speak with my lord upon that score.

"But, Pamela, my dear, you must remember it is a matter for your father's concern; not yours. You must leave everything to him, do you understand?"

Pamela's heart sang as she cried: "Oh, yes, Mama!" and threw her arms about her mother's neck.

Chapter IX

At other times and other places in the circle of London's higher Society, it may have been fashionable to be late in arriving at an affair, but where the hostess was the Dowager Duchess of Pevensey, from the highest to lowest in rank, everyone tried to be prompt. The result was a mass of congestion as the carriages lined Bloomsbury Square to await their turn at the portal of Pevensey House.

Although Pamela had never before witnessed so great a crush at any of the parties she had been privileged to attend in Surrey, still it was no more than she expected. Nor was she particularly impressed with the blaze of light that filled the place when, finally, she and her family came into the great hall of the entrance.

Geoffrey, all correct in breeches, silkstockings, and pumps, was filled with the pride of a young gentleman about to have his own establishment, and he was eager to impart the news to his chums. The Pollworths had been barely announced when he begged leave to join Kevin Fairchild. It mattered little, whether his father approved or disapproved, for he was gone like a shot, without waiting for a response.

Pamela blushed for him. They had not yet been received by the host and hostess, and she noted that her Grace whispered something to the duke behind her fan. She could have slain her brother for behaving so impetuously before their Graces.

Their turn before the duke and his mother finally came, and it fell upon Pamela to make the introductions. This she accomplished gracefully. But, to her consternation, Lady Pollworth went on to address her Grace.

"Oh, your Grace, I really must apologize for my son. There was no holding him. I assure you I shall see to it that he presents himself to you before the evening is done. It is just that he is at that age when his views of what is of importance are rather strange. I am sure you understand, your Grace, as you have had one of your own."

The duke laughed out loud, and the duchess repressed a little smile. Pamela's face turned all colors and she wished the party were over. But the next instant restored her festive feelings, because the duke bent over, saying "May I?" and took up her dance card. With the gilt, little pencil attached, he jotted down "Gerald" for the sixth set.

Pamela blushed and dipped into a curtsy, and then moved on.

Of course she was pleased, but she was not overjoyed. His Grace was condescending to notice her and nothing more. She would be his sixth partner for the evening, which made of the gesture, but a neighborly one.

However, Lady Pollworth was delighted. At their very first appearance in public, her daughter had gained the notice, and therefore the approval, of the Duke of Pevensey, something a great deal more than many of the other noble mothers would be able to boast by the time the evening was ended. Not more than a dozen young ladies would be sharing the compliment.

Pamela's searching glances about the ballroom gained her further disappointment. It was obvious to all, who were the newcomers to London. The manner of dress was quite revealing.

What with the inclement weather, there had been no chance to shop for appropriate clothes and she had had to make do with the very best that she had brought with her from Surrey. But Surrey's couturières were far and away behind the London styles, so that she might have stood out as being fresh from the country. As it was, perhaps a third of the ladies were in the same case with her. Amongst her friends, only Eleanor Fairchild had naught to complain. Her family, although as new to the Bloomsbury neighborhood as were the Pollworths, had moved there from another part of London, so that Miss Fairchild's apparel could stand comparison quite easily.

Considering that Pamela was so very sensitive with regard to the way the Pollworths ought to appear to Society, she could not feel comfortable.

She parted company with her father and mother to join her friends, and was besieged by all of them with questions as to what his Grace had said to her when he put his name down. Obviously none of them had gained such honor, and they wished to make the most of hers, demanding to see the handwriting on her card. There was some commotion as they all chatted back and forth, expressing their envy of Pamela, good-naturedly. But, even as they spoke together, young gentlemen were beginning to come up to them to sign their cards. Since Pamela had been singled out by his Grace, the greater number of them addressed their attentions to her, first.

She felt better about it all, realizing that she had been honored, and tried to give consideration to how it must reflect upon herself and her family. It was not an easy thing to do, because she was put to the trouble of maintaining a pleasant demeanor before her friends and her would-be partners at the same time.

There was some thought nagging at her, but she could not find the time to understand what it was that was bothering her until, at last, the conversation died down and the music opening the dance started up. Her first partner came to claim her for the dance, and they stood together watching his Grace open the festivities with the daughter of an earl for partner. It was a slow minuet, something Pamela could have danced in her sleep. When his Grace and the lady had performed the first figure, it was time for the others to join them on the floor. There was something absent-minded about the way Pamela allowed her partner to lead her out and commence the dance.

Although he did his best to charm her with his grace and his wit, her monosyllabic responses quickly drained him of any enthusiasm for her company, and he proceeded through the figures without further comment.

Pamela was entirely engrossed in her thoughts, performing her part colorlessly, almost unconscious of the ball that was going on about her.

It came to her, shortly before the dance ended, that she was fast approaching a situation that was deplorable. She feared that there was not sufficient time for it to be circumvented unless she took a hand in it. She could not leave it up to her mother. Her ladyship was too dilatory to be trusted.

It was the same problem that had been haunting her for some time, only now, the embarrassment the Pollworths must suffer for the lack of a French chef was imminent.

Since the duke had accorded her the privilege of dancing with him, it meant that she had received the approval of the dowager duchess and so had her family. What must follow was the usual round of entertainments to be held at the various homes in the district, and that must call for affairs to be given at Pollworth House, too. There it was! And it could be even worse!

Because of this connection with the Pevenseys, it might come about that the Pollworths would be called upon to entertain others from the very highest circles in London. What a disgrace to spread before them the boiled mutton and oatmeal puddings of Mrs. Biggams!

It would not be long before the Pollworths found themselves outcasts, their friends would drop away from them, and worst of all, she would be without an escort. She doubted if even Kevin Fairchild would be *so* gallant as to come calling upon a family, out of fashion, and beyond all acceptance by polite Society.

By the time the dance was ended and her partner fled without a word of thanks, Pamela had made up her mind to pursue her original objective at all costs. It was the perfect opportunity, and time was running out. There was a chef at hand and, although she was puzzled as to the degree of his Grace's satisfaction, she was willing to believe that it was not great. No one had ventured a taste of Monsieur Galliard's collation during her recent visit.

Making the decision to take this action was difficult, in light of her mother's expressed disapproval, but even more difficult was how to effect it. She did not have to glance at her card to see that all her dances were taken, nor did she have to remind herself that she would never hear the end of it from her mother if she failed to appear on the floor with his Grace. Yet, if she were to accomplish anything at all, it had to be done at some sacrifice. The question was: who was to be made to suffer? The answer came quickly enough. Her next partner!

Never before had she ever to excuse herself from a dance but, as necessity is the mother of invention, she managed to conceive of a most original pretext. When her second partner came for her, she explained to him that she had the headache and would have to retire upstairs for a bit until she could recover.

He turned pale, murmured something, and walked stiffly away. Pamela was too filled with her own concerns to pay any mind to him. She turned and made her way up the staircase to the first floor and proceeded to search for the backstairs.

It was such a large house that she was all of five minutes threading her way to what she believed was the rear. The corridor took her out of earshot of the cloakrooms where servants were in attendance and brought her into a wing whose existence she never had suspected. It quite confused her, and she was not sure of her direction at all. But, one thing was certain. She had not come to any other staircase at all.

Pamela had been so sure of herself up to this point that she had not marked the way she had come. She must have forgotten that the corridor branched off

126

here and there, for when she attempted to retrace her steps, she wound up in another wing, more confused than ever.

But now, her confusion was flavored with a touch of panic. The music for the second set was coming to a conclusion. If she did not return, there would be a highly indignant gentleman to whom she would have to apologize.

Panic suggested a cry for help, but logic insisted that it would be foolish indeed. How could she explain her presence so far from the ballroom? Whatever she did, she was bound to be embarrassed, and as the party was progressing, there was bound to come a time when her absence would be remarked upon and, worst of all, investigated. But what was she to do?

She began to walk hurriedly in the direction she was facing. No house could be so large that finding one's way in it was insuperable. Whether Pevensey house was that limited, she never did find out, for succor came walking spiritedly around the corner, and ran into her with a resounding "Ooof!"

It was in the shape of a little man, who recoiled agilely and cried: "Bli' me!!"

"Coo! 'T is the kine' lydy!!" he chirped, as she caught at his arm to steady herself.

Recovering quickly, she smiled and said: "Is that you, Bertie? My, how handsome you look!"

His grin of appreciation threatened to split his face as he nodded, vehemently. Then he proudly pranced about before her, thumbing his lapels and throwing out his chest. "If the lads in 'orspital could see me now, eh wot!"

He was dressed in the silks and satins of the duke's livery, but very much in miniature, of course—a tiny edition of Twemlow, which made his appearance all the more darling.

"And how is his Grace treating you, Bertie?"

"Up to the knocker, yer lydyship. 'E's a oner, 'Is Gryce is!"

"It is very nice meeting you again, Bertie, and I am gratified to see you happy in your new post. Er—can you direct me to the backstairs?"

"That Hi can, yer lydyship. Foller me if yer please."

He led her to another turning and pointed out the door that had hidden the stairs from her view. She thanked him and started down.

"Hi sy, yer lydyship, 't is the long way about to the party!" he called out, looking down over the bannister at her. "P'raps Hi better show yer the wy!"

She paused and thought a little. "Perhaps you had better, Bertie, but it is the kitchen I wish to visit. This will take me belowstairs, will it not?"

"Aye, that it will! 'T will be me pleasure, yer lydyship!"

He came scrambling down to her and took the lead.

"I suspect that Monsieur Galliard is rather busy in the kitchen at the moment and he might not care to be disturbed," she said tentatively.

" 'Oo?" he asked, looking back blankly.

"Monsieur Galliard, the duke's chef."

"Oh, that one! 'Is nibs, ol' Frenchie. 'E's a Tartar, 'e is! Hi don't like 'im one bit, Hi don't! But 'e 'ates Twemlow, an' as Hi 'ates Ol' Longshanks, too, Hi don't mind 'im all that much. Be 'im what you wishes to see?"

"Yes, I have a wish to speak with him."

"Coo! Not in 'is kitchen, yer lydyship! 'E ayn't yuman, 'e ayn't! Best Hi fetch Ol' Plunkett. 'E'll know 'ow ter deal wi' the bloke!"

128

"No, no, Bertie! I assure you it is quite all right. I just wish to have a little chat with him. Let us proceed."

"As yer wish, yer lydyship."

At her first sight of the Pevensey kitchen, Pamela let out a gasp. The place was huge, almost as large as the ballroom upstairs, she thought. And it was a veritable maze of counters and rooms, with servants running all about, through clouds of savory-smelling steam, so that there was something infernal in the impression it gave. She was thankful for her guide, for she was sure that she would have been defeated in her attempt to penetrate the reeking cavern. For one thing, she would have been too frightened to try.

She could see that more than a few cooks were at work, and it made her easier in her mind. Mrs. Biggam had but two scullery maids to assist her in the little cubicle of a kitchen which was all that the Pollworths could boast. The difference in size between the two kitchens set her to wondering whether or not Monsieur Galliard might not find her family's place too confining. But then she assured herself that he might not, for there would not be anything like the work in which he was presently involved.

She followed closely behind Bertie, who was not making very speedy progress. It struck her that, as he was quite new in the house, the vastness of the kitchen was almost as unfamiliar to him as it was to her. In any case, the air was so thick with pungent aromas and steamy vapors that her eyes watered in protest, and she could understand the difficulty Bertie might be experiencing in his attempts at identifying the various kitchen toilers.

He was stopping each one on the way and peering

into his face, demanding to be told where the Frenchie could be found. But everyone was too busy and they merely brushed him aside in their continual scurrying to and fro.

Undiscouraged, Bertie continued to advance deeper and deeper into the kitchen precincts and the air about them grew warmer as they approached the great ovens, whose roaring filled the chamber.

Pamela, to give herself heart, said to herself that if Monsieur Galliard went in for brimstone-flavoring, it would be impossible to distinguish the Pevensey kitchen from an outlying district of that Gehenna the Fundamentalist preachers wrote and lectured about.

Therefore, it was a shock when a huge personage in drooping black mustaches, advanced upon them, shaking a great wooden spoon in a most menacing fashion, shouting: "You, miette! Petite crumb! I smash you! From la cuisine, arrière! Shoo! Out, out, out!"

The chef was now towering over Bertie, his hands on his hips, feet astride, glaring down at him. Bertie impudently struck a similar pose and grinned back up at him. At that point, the chef realized that a lady was present and, at once, he was all smiles, bowing as gracefully as his great girth would permit.

"Ah, mam'selle, I did not see you at firs'. It is the great pleasure to 'ave you visit Hippolyte in 'eez kee-shen! I am so ver' pleased! 'Ow can I serve you, mam'selle?"

Bertie nodded approvingly and remarked: "We expects a civil tongue in yer fyce, me good man! See that yer remembers it!"

Galliard began to fume, and Pamela advised Bertie to leave her. She thanked him for his assistance, and went on to say that she wished to speak in confidence to Monsieur Galliard.

At this, the Frenchman smiled nastily at Bertie, who answered him with an outthrust tongue, before he skipped away.

Galliard's face renewed the extreme expression of pleasure and he asked: "To me you 'ave come to speak? Ah, I am flattered. Come, I show you how the great Hippolyte cooks for the great Duch de Pevensey."

Before she could reject his invitation, he had moved off to one of the ranges, where a younger man, in a costume similar to his own, was wrestling with a great copper pan. He was busy stirring a golden-yellow mixture, that gave off a tantalizing, lemony aroma.

Galliard came over to him, made a sign for him to cease his toil and thrust his spoon into the pan. Taking up a bit of the contents, he said: "You taste, mam'selle", and his eyes lit up in anticipation of her comment.

Pamela would have preferred not to have done so, but she thought that refusing would be a poor way to begin to win him over to her scheme. She took the spoon from him and shyly brought it to her lips.

It was warm, it was rich, it was tangy, and it was incredibly smooth. It was unlike anything she had ever tasted, and she could hardly believe it was food.

"Oh, monsieur, it is delectable!" she exclaimed, and she helped herself to another taste.

Galliard, his eyes popping with delight and pride, nodded vigorous agreement, and handed the pan back to his assistant. That luckless fellow placed it back on the low fire, evincing a scream of outrage from the chef.

He realized his mistake at once, and snatched the pan off the range. But it was too late to stem the torrent of Gallic oaths that Galliard rained down upon his head.

"Vache! Cochon! Idiot! To put ze Sauce Hollandaise into ze fire after I, Hippolyte Galliard, chef extraodinaire, say it is finie! Merde! It is a sauce, stupide, not pouding anglais! It is not to be boiled—but gently, and only just so!"

By this time, the miscreant had scurried away to busy himself at a far counter. Galliard was still shaking the spoon at him as he turned to Pamela.

To calm him, she thought to change the subject. "It is then a Dutch sauce, monsieur?" she asked politely.

"Non, non, mam'selle! Nevair for a moment is it a Dush sauce. From the Dush, it comes, but it is dull. It is boring! We French 'ave made of it a delight supreme, and so it becomes the Sauce Hollandaise, comprendez-vous?"

"How interesting! I am so glad that I came to visit you, monsieur."

"And I am so delighted to 'ave you visit mon cuisine. It is not like your English kee-shens, n' est-ce pas?"

"Oh, not at all, monsieur, and it makes me long to find such a one as you for our kitchen. All we have got is an Englishwoman, and she knows naught but our old-fashioned English cooking. She has lived all her life in the country and would never dream of attempting to prepare anything as delicious as what I have just tasted."

First, Galliard looked shocked, and then he looked sad. He shook his head in pity, and said: "Ah, ma belle pauvre, how do you live? C'est exécrable! You would like for to find a chef français, eh?"

"Oh, mais oui, monsieur! Do you have a suggestion, perhaps?"

"Ah, mam'selle, des chefs in England is not many. I do not know," he said, sorrowfully. "Your family, she is wealthy, yes?" His heavy, black eyebrows leaped skywards.

Pamela's heart leaped, too. Obviously, she was on the right track with him. Very soberly, she said: "Oh, yes, monsieur. We can easily afford a better table than we are now enjoying. And, although we Pollworths are not dukes and duchesses, still a proper French chef would be royally treated in our establishment. Are you quite sure you have no suggestions to make to me?"

"At the moment, mam'selle, non! I must think about it, firs'! You would like someone, grand et bon, like Hippolyte Galliard, pairhops?"

If his eyebrows had been eye lashes, one might have said they were fluttering as he asked the question.

Pamela, unheeding, replied: "I am sure we would be honored to have *you* in our service, monsieur."

"Ah, so I 'ave been t'inking. You are too kind, mam'selle. Now, I have ze food to prepare. I go."

He turned on his heel and marched away through the pungent steam, leaving Pamela with the strong feeling that she had misjudged her man. All she could do for the moment was to stand and stare after him.

"Miss Pollworth, what the devil are you doing in my kitchen?" demanded a highly irate voice behind her.

She gasped and wheeled about, to face the Duke of Pevensey.

Chapter X

She stood, facing him, her mind and tongue incapable of putting together any reasonable answer.

"Miss Pollworth, are you out to embarrass me? This was our dance, if you will be so kind as to consult your card. I could not believe my ears when, from Bertie of all people, I gained the information that you had descended to the kitchen. I still find it hard to credit it. I am waiting, Miss Pollworth, for some explanation. Was it Galliard you had a wish to speak with?"

To give herself time to think, Pamela made a pretense of looking at the card which was dangling from her wrist. "Heavens, how the time must have flown. Your Grace, of course I must offer you my humblest apologies. It is truly time for our set to commence?"

"It is well past, I should say," he returned curtly.

"Oh dear, I do not know what to say! I would not have missed our dance for anything, your Grace. Whatever are we to do?"

"Miss Pollworth, I suspect that your interview with Galliard superseded all other considerations with you. I beg you not to deny it, for I have it upon Twemlow's authority that it was Galliard—or something connected with him, that brought you to my door in the first place. Now, I would treat one riddle at a time, and it has been a bother to me, the reason for your first appearance in this house. You did come to speak with Galliard, did you not?"

"Your Grace, you are not to think that there was anything exceptional in my coming to interview a person who was a perfect stranger to me. I mean to say—"

"You do not have explain to me, Miss Pollworth. I am sure I know the sorry tale. It is nothing new, except that the business usually involves someone older, a matron, in rare instances, a gentleman of family. How does it come about that your mother sends so young a lady, to try to steal my chef from me?"

Pamela's face blushed crimson. "Your Grace, I would not have you think ill of my lady mother. I do assure you it was entirely my own idea—but I pray you will not think too ill of me. It was not to *steal* your chef that I came into your kitchen. I had heard that you and he were not on the best of terms. I would have offered him a more appreciative master."

"Miss Pollworth, this is no place to go into the business. Do you see in yon corner, my cherished Hippolyte waving his eyebrows at us? I have enough trouble with the fellow, he is in such demand. Come. I venture to say that our absence has been already noted and there will be talk. I do not see that we can amend the business by rushing out upon the dance floor, looking as guilty as sin; therefore, I suggest that you join me in my study and I shall send for the dowager to chaperone us. There will still be talk, but it will never be so scandalous. I have a notion that the Lady Charlotte has a burning curiosity to satisfy, with regard to you, my dear."

"Th-the Lady Charlotte? Must we?"

"I do not see any other choice. We shall at least be able to make our appearance in her company, thus stilling the worst of the gossips' tongues. Of course, it is bound to play hob with my dance program and with yours, Miss Pollworth, but I imagine you are capable of making your own excuses. I know I shall have a devil of a time making my own!"

The duchess came sailing into the study and her eyes were ablaze with anger.

"Gerald, this is shocking beyond limit! And you, Miss Pollworth, I should think you would know better! Can you imagine what is being said out on the floor? Oh, how I suffer! I try to do a neighborly turn, and what do I receive? Scandal! Gerald, we have got a scandal on our hands. I fear that this party will be a subject for the nastiest gossip of the Season!"

Pamela shrank back in her chair, but the duke arose and said: "Madam, I am quite aware of the difficulties of the situation, and it is why I have sent for you. I am sure that, with your cooperation, the business can be mitigated, if not entirely put to rest."

"I never said it could not, Gerald, but I must say, it comes as a surprise to me, your mother, that you should do this senseless thing—"

"I pray you will cease your recriminations and give ear to me. We have here naught but what has occurred many times, since we engaged Hipployte to cook for us."

The duchess had found herself a seat and was now

137

regarding Pamela with a look of surprise. "This one, too? Heavens, and she is not even married! My girl, whatever is on your mind? What do you intend to do with a chef?"

"He was not intended for me, in particular, your Grace. I had understood that Monsieur Galliard was not satisfied with his employment and would entertain an offer from another establishment. My understanding was in error, it seems."

"And you selected this time for chef-shopping? Is that where you discovered her, Gerald? In the kitchen?"

"Aye," assented the duke. "I should never have guessed but for the fact that it was my tiger who conducted her there. Actually, I should have suspicioned it after what Twemlow related to me."

"Twemlow? What has he to say to anything? How is it that he did not bring his information to me? Gerald, what is going on? You are subverting my very own servants. I tell you I do not like it one bit. I have half a mind to leave for Pevensey and let you see what it is to run this great house."

He laughed. "If that threat is supposed to reduce me to a veritable jelly of quaking fear, Mama, consider it done; but, in the meantime, we have got more important matters to discuss. I take it, Miss Pollworth, you did manage to have your little chat with Hippolyte, did you not?"

"Yes, your Grace."

"If I am not intruding upon an employer-employee relationship, I should be gratified to learn in detail what was the outcome."

"There was none. When I did suggest he come to work for my family, he walked away."

"Good old Hippolyte. His loyalty is so flattering to

one. I pray you were not too disappointed, Miss Pollworth. Monsieur Galliard is very expensive. Even as a duke I feel the strain of his hands upon my purse."

"Oh dear!" exclaimed Pamela. "Are all of them so very expensive, your Grace? I do not think that my father would be happy to have to pay such wages, after Mrs. Biggam."

"Aha! So it was your father who has put you up to this piracy, is it?" snapped her Grace. "I cannot understand how the times can have changed so much. Gerald, I must say this is unheard of: a peer to send his own daughter out upon such a mission as this."

"Oh no, your Grace!" protested Pamela, very upset. "I do assure you, my Lord Pollworth knows nothing of any of this!"

"Not for long shall he remain in ignorance if I have my say," declared the duchess.

"I pray you will go slowly, your Grace," cautioned the duke. "I have the strangest feeling that what is about to follow will be less than flattering to me, but I would that Miss Pollworth explain, precisely, why she feels the need of a Frenchman in her family's kitchen."

"Your Grace, this is foolishness beyond belief," rejoined the duchess. "What of our guests? Whilst we sit here, prosing on and on about the reprehensible behavior of Miss Pollworth, there is neither host nor hostess present at the Duke of Pevensey's ball. Shall we even be in time to take leave of them?"

"I am sure we shall, Mama. It would be in the poorest form for them to leave, otherwise; would it not? Now then, Miss Pollworth, I am slowly coming to the conclusion that I, myself, was not the greatest attraction that brought you to the party this evening."

"Oh, but of course, your Grace. You are a duke, and it is a privilege and an honor to have been invited to the party, I do assure you."

"I see. Then it was not so great a thing to have that dance with me. I mean to say that your business with Hippolyte was of more moment."

"I do regret your having got that notion, your Grace. Of course, it is of the first importance that we get us a French chef, but I did not think it would have taken so long. Are you quite sure that our dance is over? It seemed to me that no time at all had elapsed."

"I fear I do not quite understand, Miss Pollworth. You say that this matter of a chef is of the first importance. To whom, may I ask?"

"Your Grace, all pardon, but it is not a topic a young lady cares to discuss."

"Gerald, what are you getting at? I have the distinct feeling that I am sitting in a court of law!" declared the duchess. "Please have done with it, and tell me how we are to smooth the business over before all the world."

"A moment, Mama. I am finding this conversation quite fascinating. Miss Pollworth, you are amongst friends, and I can hardly believe that there is anything you have to say that you need blush for."

Pamela was reluctant to go into it. She hesitated, while she gazed at the duke. She thought him particularly handsome, as he sat in an easy attitude before her. There was an arrogant air about him at the moment, yet he was smiling sweetly at her. She decided that, as matters stood, perhaps she owed him some explanation for the embarrassment she was causing all concerned.

"It is nothing I need be ashamed of, your Grace. The fact is that my father will not have a French cook of any sort in the house. He is more than content with the dishes that Mrs. Biggam prepares. But all my friends' families have French chefs and it seemed to me that we would make a very poor appearance before our friends and neighbors if our table continued to be so out-of-fashion. I am getting on in years and do hope to marry. An eligible gentleman might take exception to me if he found that my family was not up to snuff in such a matter. I do apologize for having sought your cook out, but then, I did not know that you set any store upon him. I noticed that you never even tasted of that collation he prepared when I called upon you—and I was *dying* to sample it!"

"I do declare!" exclaimed her Grace.

The duke laughed loudly and turned to his mother. "As I live and breathe, your Grace, it would appear that we have been guilty of bad manners before Miss Pollworth. Pehaps the score between us is dead-even."

"Gerald, I am so embarrassed. Of course, I remember it now. Galliard had gone to greater pains than I had thought necessary, but the young lady is quite right. I never did offer anything to her. How bad of me! Oh, Miss Pollworth, I do extend my apologies to you—but then I do not understand why you were so intent upon Galliard if you had not tasted of his cooking."

"Oh, but I have, your Grace," replied Pamela, feeling much happier that the atmosphere had lightened. "He let me have a taste of that marvelous Dutch sauce of his. Oh, I wish we could afford someone like him!"

"Ah, the Hollandaise, the devil! Leave it to Hippolyte to make hay!" exclaimed the duke, jovially. "I say, Mama, what was it he tempted Lady Oxley with?"

At the recollection, her Grace was smiling, too. "I do

141

believe that it was gâteau des pommes. Poor dear Lady Oxley, she chose a bad moment. It is such a delicate and tasty morsel, and the cook she finally ended up with, has not the recipe. I dare say she envies me no end—but, as you say, Hippolyte does deal harshly with our friends who would try to spirit him away from us."

"So, Miss Pamela, you do not think that you would be very successful in finding yourself a husband lest you had a French chef. Is that correct?"

"I know you are laughing at me, your Grace, but you must admit a proper chef would make it a deal easier."

The Lady Charlotte looked sharply at her son and raised an eyebrow.

"Indeed, I am well told," he said, and laughed. Then he sighed. "Your Grace, I do not see that we can extend this conversation further with any profit. Will you be good enough to accompany us back to our guests? It will not be exceptional if we let it be known that Miss Pamela is an old friend and we have been at reminiscing, all apologies to everyone for our thoughtlessness. Miss Pamela, will that be suitable, do you think?"

"Oh yes, your Grace. All my friends think it is so. You did not ask any of them to dance, but you did me."

"Yes," he drawled. "Perhaps I should have had better luck if I had," he concluded ruefully.

If the Duke of Pevensey's affair did nothing more for the inhabitants of Mecklenburg Square, it provided them with a date of reference so that they could conveniently calendar subsequent events. It rapidly became the practice to respond: "Ah, yes, such and such occurred three days after his Grace's affair."

To the surprise of her friends, Pamela was not at all elated. In fact, following that notable event, her spirits declined markedly, so much so that Eleanor Fairchild commented upon it to her mother.

"Mama, it is the strangest thing, but ever since the duke's party, Pamela Pollworth has been in the lowest of spirits. Considering all the attention she garnered from his Grace and the duchess, one would think that she would be in alt forever. But no, it is not the case with her. I truly do not understand it. The duke is such a charming fellow, I, for one, would be happy if he merely condescended to smile upon me."

Lady Fairchild replied: "My dear, I am not so sure that all is as it appears on the surface. We know, do we not, that the Pollworths and the Lyttons do not go back very far together. They are from Surrey and their Graces' seat is in Sussex. Although that may be close enough to warrant an acquaintanceship, it is rare that his Grace is absent from London; whereas the dowager, I am willing to wager, hardly ever stirs out of Bloomsbury Square, except to attend some exclusive function. I find it hard to credit what we were told.

"No, child, there is something strange in it. The very fact that his Grace and Pamela did not have their dance together speaks volumes, I must say."

"But volumes of what, Mama? Pamela says nothing out of the ordinary occurred, and she *will* stick by her story that it was just a friendly meeting. Do you think there will be other invitations to Pevensey House?"

"Love, I have not the slightest idea. I have tried to get some indication from Lady Pollworth, but she seems to be as puzzled over it all, as are the rest of us. Of course, it could be that she does not wish to disclose anything. There is that to be considered."

"But what can there be to hide?" persisted Eleanor.

Lady Fairchild merely shrugged her shoulders, and they went on to speak of other things.

It was quite true. Pamela was dispirited, and although it did not help matters in the least, Lord Pollworth was angry.

His lordship was also as puzzled as all the rest, and being a gentleman who put a premium on everything being plain and simple, his daughter's refusal, or inability, to make things plain and simple to him, kept him in a state of elevated choler for days after the party. He made complaint to his lady, and he made complaint to his daughter, but nothing they said to him served to relieve his discomfort with the situation.

"It is disgraceful, I tell you, Constance, that we should have this embarrassment thrust upon us. By heaven, if he was something less than a duke, I should go right over to Bloomsbury Square and demand an explanation from his Grace."

"Yes, dear, but precisely what would you demand of him? I see that Pamela is upset about something, and the business of her being with the duke and his mother during so much of the party was strange; but as it was nothing to take exception to, it hardly seems fitting for you to demand of the gentleman an explanation. If you will recall, he did explain, as did her Grace, and it was all so very complimentary to Pamela."

"Aye, there's the puzzle! Why then is our daughter so unhappy of late? No, there has got to be a better explanation than what was given, I tell you."

"Frederick, whatever it is, I have no doubt that in good time, all will be revealed."

"Fiddlesticks, my love! It is what you always say."

"And I am always right, you will admit."

There was a pained look upon Lord Pollworth's face as he grunted, and walked out of the room.

Pamela did not see that her meeting with their Graces had solved her problem. If anything, it had only made matters worse. If the Lyttons were about to take her into their circle as a dear friend, then the time would come when courtesy must prompt her mother to tender an invitation to them to come to dine. But, well before that might occur, there would be other invitations, and Pollworth House might well be inundated by guests and callers of high rank. The thought that these grand and great people would be offered only the limited and unfashionable dishes from Mrs. Biggam's repertory made her feel quite blue. The Pollworth family's credit before the world of high fashion would suffer irretrievably.

It was no use of her making any further appeal to her mother. Lady Pollworth was in alt over the prospect of her future entertainments. She no longer gave ear to her daughter's complaints of Mrs. Biggam. She was sure that their acceptance by the Lyttons was all that was needed to guarantee their entrée into the most exalted realms of Society.

As for her father, she found that these days, it was best to stay out of his way as much as possible. Trying to convince him of Mrs. Biggam's failings she knew to be impossible. If she were ever to gain her way in the matter of the Pollworth's cuisine, it would have to be in an indirect manner. It would have to be of the nature of a fait accompli before his lordship could forbid it. The foreign phrase, that fitted her thought so neatly, gave her a sense of confidence and served to confirm her in her determination.

But is was one thing to make a resolution to continue in her efforts to replace Mrs. Biggam, and quite another to discover the way to accomplish it. She had had only Monsieur Galliard to consider before. Now, she must seek out some perfect French stranger and begin all over again. As she was under the strictest orders never to leave the house in the future without a maid and footman to escort her, the magnitude of her difficulty could easily be estimated.

When her mother received a note from the Duchess of Pevensey indicating that great lady's desire to make a call in the company of the duke, Pamela felt quite defeated. Although her Grace was aware of the state of the Pollworth's kitchen, the visit signaled the beginning of the end for Pamela's prospects.

Chapter XI

Until the day, the hour, almost the instant of the arrival, of their Graces, the Pollworth household was a maelstrom of activity, and at the center, and perhaps the cause, of all the turmoil was Lady Pollworth. Although the house had been newly decorated, it suddenly appeared to her to be drab and unattractive. Interminable debates arose over the suitability of furnishings to which, but weeks ago, her ladyship had given her blessing with pride and joy. But, as she pointed out, she had never had it in mind to entertain dukes, obviously, a finer and more expensive decor was called for by such an august presence.

Lord Pollworth was in a way to profit heavily from Bonaparte's declining fortunes on the Continent, and so his objections to this added expenditure were not maintained with any great vigor. In fact, as the appointment drew near, and the hectic pace of his household grew ever more frenzied, he discovered a refuge in his club, and managed to convince himself that his presence before the duke and her Grace, was not all that necessary.

Lady Pollworth was not destroyed to hear his decision to be absent, but Pamela was filled with envy. She was not looking forward to any further meetings with the Lyttons, and wished profoundly that she were back in Surrey.

Despite her unhappiness over the great honor that was about to befall the family, Pamela worked along with her mother to make the house fitting in all respects. She tempered many of her mother's wilder suggestions with reason, and saw to it that the serving staff did not have to stand about, puzzling over the vague instructions they received from the mistress of the house.

Finally everything was set in order. With the exception of Lord Pollworth, family and serving staff were fully prepared for the coming trial. His lordship went to the trouble of explaining more than once the demands upon his time and urged his lady to make profuse apologies to their Graces for his inability to be present to make them welcome. Her ladyship assured him that he was not to worry, he would not be missed. This was not quite what Lord Pollworth had wished to hear, but in the interest of family peace, upon the eve of so great an event, he refrained from further comment.

There was a certain charm about Lady Pollworth, and a part of it was due to the fact that she was never at a loss for conversation. Even the exalted rank of the duke and duchess could not stem her urge to speak, and so, when all the little ceremony of greeting them was done with, she went right off into a paean of praise for the wonderful affair that their Graces had been responsible for.

However, the duchess had a liking for a conversation in which she took some part, and at the first opportunity—a pause for breath by Lady Pollworth, managed to interject the remark: "Pamela informs us that you are on the lookout for a chef, Lady Pollworth. How are you progressing?"

The question caught Lady Pollworth completely at sea. She was not sufficiently well acquainted with her Grace to contemplate discussing her domestic affairs with her, and, furthermore, she was baffled for the moment to understand how the duchess knew that there had been any discussion of a chef in the Pollworth domicile. And, even beyond that, except that her Grace was her Grace, such an inquiry from one who was practically a total stranger would have been an outright impertinence. It was a rare moment for Lady Pollworth to find herself at a loss for words.

Pamela hurried to her rescue by responding: "It is old business with us, your Grace. We prefer to gloss over the matter."

The duke smiled quizzically and asked: "Are you then satisfied with Mrs. Biggam?"

Lady Pollworth could only sit and stare at her daughter like a wounded bird. Pamela had, apparently, let out all the family secrets to strangers. But loyalty to her household gave her breath, and she rushed to its defense.

"I assure you, your Grace, we are now more than satisfied with Mrs. Biggam. She has been with us for years and I am sure that Lord Pollworth would miss her good cooking if we were to lose her."

"Indeed, Lady Pollworth, it is gratifying to learn. So many families have much to complain, of late, about their culinary staffs. It is quite the topic of conversation these days, putting to rout others that one might consider more preferable." He shot a glance at Pamela.

The conversation then went off at a tangent, involving the duchess and Lady Pollworth, mainly; leaving Pamela to ponder over his Grace's cryptic remark. She sensed a reproach to herself in it, and quickly concluded that he was remarking upon her bad taste in invading his house, to have a conversation with one of his servants without his permission.

She took umbrage at his reprimand, considering that she had admitted her error, and had begged his pardon. She did not think it fair of him to harp on it. He ought, if he had forgiven her, to have forgotten it. As he had not done the latter, it was obvious he had not done the former either. She was sure that, if this were to prove to be her last sight of his Grace, she would not be overwhelmed with grief.

Gibbs, the Pollworth butler made his appearance in the doorway, and Lady Pollworth nodded to him. He bowed and withdrew.

Said Lady Pollworth to her visitors: "I have had a small collation prepared. I pray you will partake of it. I assure you it is good English cookery."

The Lady Charlotte's lips twisted a little, but she left it to her son to reply.

"I am sure her Grace and I are looking forward to what must be a treat. However, Lady Pollworth, I ought to point out that we Lyttons are not strangers to the fare of our native land. In fact, I pride myself on the fact that my chef, be he ever so French, can prepare the dishes of any number of nations, ours included."

Pamela expressed surprise. "If that is the case, your Grace, why must he be a Frenchman? He might just as well be an Italian, or—or —"

"Or an Englishman, even a Mrs. Biggam, perhaps? But of course. Nationality has nothing to say as to the excellence of a cook. You may call him chief cook, chef, or *capo cuoco,* it makes no difference. If the blighter can cook, even his sex has naught to say to it—if you know what I mean. I am sure that Mrs. Biggam must be a most excellent cook."

"It is so kind of you to say so, your Grace," chimed in Lady Pollworth, "and you have not had even a taste of one of her dishes. But do not despair. Gibbs will be serving us soon."

As soon as the trays were carried into the room, everyone was aware that an error had been made, even Lady Pollworth. There was an aroma of roses pervading the room which, under other circumstances might have been pleasant as incense, but was far too overwhelming as a flavoring.

Immediately, Lady Pollworth was all apologies. "Oh dear, it escaped me, and poor, dear Mrs. Biggam neglected to inform me. I had forgot that each of the dishes had rosewater for an ingredient. You see, there on the table are collared eels—which, of course, have a variety of spices in them, but not rosewater. I dare say it is from the saffron bread and the biscuits. I thought one might have wished a bit of butter on the biscuits—they are warm, you know—and the saffron bread makes the most excellent toast—for those who might prefer toast—that is. But, now that I think of it, they neither of them would go awfully well with collared eels, do you think? Naughty, naughty Mrs. Biggam. I am sure she knows better than this."

She looked at the duke, and then to the duchess, her features a picture of misery. Pamela's heart was broken for her mother. Yes, a proper chef would never have let such an assortment of dishes out of his kitchen—but she had been expecting something like this, sooner or later, and so was prepared for the embarrassment, as her mother was not.

Bravely, she took it upon herself to suggest that the dishes be returned and something more to their Graces' liking, be prepared. She was not at all particularly surprised to see the duchess rise and politely decline. There was a pained expression on the duke's countenance as he jumped to his feet, exclaiming: "How quickly time passes in pleasant company!"

The ritual of their departure was, thankfully, brief, for they had no sooner left then Lady Pollworth's tears, no longer repressed, gushed down her cheeks, as she complained: "Oh, what have I done! Child, I do believe I have ruined everything! Oh, that horrid Mrs. Biggam!"

If there had been a chef in the offing at that particular moment, Pamela could have rejoiced, for she knew her mother would have stood with her, against her father, on the question. But it was too late, the damage had been done—and she knew not where to turn to find a proper chef to repair it, if it were at all possible.

She took her mother in her arms and commiserated with her. They came back into the heavily rose-scented room to plan a campaign to convince Lord Pollworth that London was not for them. They had lost their entrée into the Duchess of Pevensey's set, and could now consider themselves pariahs in the city. They should never have left Surrey in the first place—not without a French chef in tow!

Chapter XII

That evening, when Lord Pollworth returned to the bosom of his family, that fragile domestic peace, he so much cherished, was not to be had. Instead, he was greeted with tears, and the wringing of hands, to give dramatic emphasis to the tale of social horror that swiftly followed.

He was not so blind as not to appreciate the failings of the family cook and how they had contributed to the utter ruin of the Pollworths in the eyes of the Lyttons, but he was the lord and master of the house and mustered to his defense his own reasons for continuing on in Bloomsbury, despite social disapproval. His reasons not only went to support his own determination, but they also worked to disguise his own guilty feelings.

"My dear Constance, truly I regret that you should have suffered this embarrassment, but you must recall that it was never my intention, and I pray it was never your understanding, that we were removing to London so that we might disport ourselves with dukes and duchesses. I am merely a baron, and I am quite content with my lot. Surely, you must remember that our purpose in coming into the city was, first and foremost, so that I could keep a wary eye upon the family's fortunes.

"It is a fact that I never was better advised in my life. Napoleon's star is fast setting, and my being on the scene, as it were, has allowed me to add handsomely to my holdings. It is a most glorious thing what England, with but a handful of allies, has been able to achieve against that monster, a far more glorious thing than any Duke or Duchess of Pevensey could ever hope—"

"Frederick, that is not the point at all, and you know it is not!" retorted Lady Pollworth. "We have a lovely daughter to provide for. It is all very well and good of you to go to work to raise the Pollworths' fortunes, but that is, in the end, for Geoffrey's sake. Pamela's best hope is an advantageous marriage, and London is the best place in the world for her to find the right gentleman. Why, you said as much yourself, when your first introduced the topic of our removal to the city. Then I ask you, how are we to do anything at all for our lovely daughter if we cannot prepare a proper table for our guests? Just because you are in love with Mrs. Biggam's cookery is not to say that anyone else is. Oh, you should have been here this afternoon! It was so utterly embarrassing—and do not expect *me* to know how to plan a proper London feast! I know what is expected of our station in Surrey, but here in the city everything moves at such a fearful pace, there is no keeping up with it. I tell you,

Frederick, we cannot stay on in London longer!"

Lord Pollworth blew out his cheeks. "My dear, it is not a choice we have. We *must* stay on. You are quite right when you say that things move quickly. It is precisely why I have to be here, to catch the opportunities as they appear. They do not stay for very long, and they are missed completely by the slowtop.

"As for Mrs. Biggam, I am sure that there are more than a few families from the country, yes, even from Surrey, who would find her dishes most appetizing. That they are not dukes and duchesses is just something we shall have to bear up under. Pamela will find someone, I assure you—What, did you think that this young Pevensey was for her? What nonsense! And, furthermore, in any affair of the heart, it takes more than a distaste for a particular sort of cooking to bar a match—"

"Frederick, that is not what I was thinking at all! Only, how much easier for Pamela it would have been, to have found an eligible gentleman in the Lyttons' set than our own."

"It does not hurt to marry an eligible gentleman from her own set. I say! There is this Kevin Fairchild. Now, he is a well setup young chap, and he will come into a barony, too. I do not know Lord Fairchild to speak to, but I should not hesitate if there were any thing to be gained from speaking with him. If it is your wish, I will call upon his lordship the first thing and see what can be arranged."

"Oh, you go too fast! I am sure that Pamela is not in a way to being married soon, not in London. What do you suppose will be said of us after today? It would be but to heap one embarrassment upon another to broach the topic with Lord Fairchild—besides, Pamela has not given one sign that she has an interest in Kevin."

"If it is not to be Kevin, then it is bound to be

157

someone else. London is a big city. I suggest you give it a little time. Once we have done for Bonaparte, everything will be in excellent order, and I shall be able to devote all my time and attention to you. I mean to say, I have done marvelously well for Geoffrey, and there is no reason for my not doing as well for my only daughter. Patience, patience, my sweet. We have barely settled in."

"That is what I am trying to explain to you, Frederick. Before matters go from bad to worse, we should remove ourselves back to Surrey. You do not have to come with us until your business affairs are settled—"

"What, Woman! Do you think I am made of money! I cannot be expected to maintain the strain of two establishments. Constance, I do assure you, your comfort, and that of Pamela, was my first consideration. Bloomsbury is a choice spot. It is an excellent address and it is convenient to the city. I say, why do you not go into town and do some shopping? Perhaps you have been cooped up in the house too long, you and Pamela. Dukes and duchesses are not the only interesting people to be found in London."

"Frederick—"

He raised his hand in a command for silence. "Now then, Constance, my dear, I have said all that I am going to say upon the subject. We are not going back to Surrey, and you and your daughter will just have to get used to it. My mind is made up. If I did not think that we should be quite comfortable here in Bloomsbury, I should not hesitate for a moment to do as you ask; but it is not the case, I know this better than you."

He gave a firm nod to his head and walked out.

Lady Pollworth sighed. "There is no talking with him, when he is in this mood. I had better give things time. He is bound to come round—and then, too, Pamela just might find someone of her own standing. She is only the daughter of a baron. What have we to do with dukes and duchesses? Frederick is right."

On the following day, neither Lady Pollworth, nor Pamela, was in a mood to receive callers. They both required a little time to think things over, to come to a determination as to how they were to proceed.

It was obvious that after the embarrassment that arose during their visit, they would not be hearing from the Lyttons again. As for the people who lived in the square with them, perhaps, if they were very particular of whom they chose to associate with, their lack of a fancy chef would be overlooked—which was not to say that they would not go to work with Mrs. Biggam. Something had to be done in her direction if they were to do any entertaining at all.

In Surrey, there had been no French chefs. All the better families, there, had competent cooks in their kitchens, and of them all, Mrs. Biggam had not been the least. Yes, there was something that could be accomplished with Mrs. Biggam that would be sufficient to their needs, so long as they kept them modest and avoided having to entertain their betters. Still, it was not a happy prospect they faced, at least for as long as they remained in London. So it was that Lady Pollworth and her daughter reluctantly resigned themselves to Lord Pollworth's dictation.

Early in the afternoon, mother and daughter had reached a point in their discussions where, having settled it that there was no recourse, they began to seek in what directions they might look to broaden their social horizons.

Lady Pollworth was saying: ". . . then if that be the case, my dear, we shall have to look farther afield than Bloomsbury Square. I was sure that Kevin Fairchild was a perfect young gentleman, and I could swear he was nursing a tendre for you—"

"It is not that I dislike Kevin. Of course, if he would still ask me out, I should not refuse; but, as I am not planning to become engaged to him, I shall have need of more than one caller, don't you see? Heavens, if I were to be seen with Kevin continually, I would never have any chance of meeting anyone else."

"Quite so. Perhaps, your father can be of help. After all, it is all due to him that we are in this quandary. He has many business associates, and it stands to reason that some of them must have sons, eligible young gentlemen—"

"Yes, and there is Geoffrey, too. He will be meeting many new people. Papa says that his post as secretary to the Marquess of Breyton can be a most influential one. He is bound to move in other circles—"

"But of course, my dear. Now why did I not think of that? The Marquess of Breyton must have a son. True, he would never become a duke, but—"

"Oh, Mama, let us not go through that business again!" exclaimed Pamela.

"But surely, my dear, it would not hurt to look into *Debrett's*—Yes, Gibbs, what is it?" she asked of the butler, who had come into the room.

"Your ladyship, we are having a bit of trouble in the kitchen."

"Trouble? What sort of trouble, Gibbs?"

"It is a foreign gentleman, madam. According to Mrs. Biggam, he came round to the servants' entrance and thrust himself inside. Then he pushed her aside and began to make preparations for dinner. When

160

Cook remonstrated with him, he came after her with a cleaver. I beg your pardon, madam. I would have spared you this shocking news, but that I do believe that Mrs. Biggam is quite prepared to leave your ladyship's service."

"I do not understand a word of this. What of you? What of the footmen? Surely, between the four of you, you can manage to evict this horrid person!"

The butler coughed lightly behind his hand. "It is not for lack of trying, madam. The fellow is quite mad, and has a veritable armory at his command. I fear it will take greater strength than we can muster to subdue him. I myself but narrowly escaped with my life when he thrust a huge knife at me. Madam, I beg leave to call in the Runners."

"What, and wait about while this madman cuts our throats? Nonsense, send the fellow to me!"

Gibbs' eyes opened wide. "Your ladyship, are you quite sure that it is wise? I mean to say that he is quite the wildest, most savage—"

"Do as I bid you! I shall not stand for any madmen in my house and you may tell him so!"

"I-I am not sure that this person will heed you, your ladyship, but I shall relay your wishes to him."

"Before you go, did he give his name? I should like to know with whom I am dealing."

"As he was, from the outset, in a perpetual rage, your ladyship, and as he is plagued with a foreign accent, all I could make out was Plite Gayard—"

"But it cannot be the same!" cried Pamela. "Hippolyte Galliard, is that his name?"

"It sounds very much like it, Miss Pamela."

"You have heard of this person, child?" queried Lady Pollworth.

"Oh, Mama, I am sure it cannot be the same, but

161

that is the name of the Duke of Pevensey's chef! I actually met him that one time, and spoke with him, too."

"If that is how he behaves, I cannot blame his Grace for turning him out; but that is no reason for him to come to us and terrify our good cook. Gibbs, send this creature to me at once!"

"Mama, it *is* Monsieur Galliard!" exclaimed Pamela as that worthy came striding into the room, already dressed in his great white apron and his black tocque. He was caressing the ever-present great spoon to his breast as he cried: "Mille pardons, madame! Mille pardons, madame!"

Then he turned to Pamela. "Ah, la belle mam'selle! 'Is excellency, Monseigneur le duc presents mysel', Hippolyte Galliard, chef extraordinaire, to you, mam'-selle—" he paused for an instant, his forehead corrugating with the effort of his thinking—"Mais oui! 'E presents me to you wiz 'is compliments! Zat is ver' good, n'est-ce pas?"

"Yes, the fellow *is* as mad as a hatter!" declared Lady Pollworth. "Pamela, do you understand any of his nonsense?"

"I am not sure that I do. Monsieur, why should his Grace send you to me?"

The chef grinned broadly, exclaimed: "Oh-la-la!" and kissed the tips of his fingers to her.

Declared Lady Pollworth: "The man is an utter lunatic!"

Gibbs, who was standing just inside the door and looking very nervous, said: "If your ladyship wishes, I believe we can manage to evict the fellow, now that he is disarmed."

Galliard turned and sneered: "For you, I do not give
162

this much!" and he snapped his fingers at Gibbs with contempt.

"Mama, I think that we ought to hear what Monsieur Galliard has to say for himself," Pamela said.

Lady Pollworth nodded. "I suppose we must, although I cannot imagine that he is capable of making the least sense. You, sir, what on earth are you doing here? Do you realize that I shall be losing my cook because of you?"

"Oh, non, non, madame!" exclaimed Galliard, bowing and grinning at each lady in turn. "You 'ave ze chef, you do not need ze cook."

"You are actually going to work in our kitchen?" asked Pamela.

"Mais oui, mam'selle! For why does Hippolyte Galliard come to you?"

"I really do not know, and that is why we are asking you, my good man," retorted Lady Pollworth, with some asperity in her tone.

"Madame, it is ver' simple. I, Hippolyte Galliard, come to you for to cook wiz ze compliments of monseigneur le duc, n'est-ce pas?"

Her ladyship looked indignant. "Do you not know?"

"Oui, I, Hippolyte Galliard, know. It is madame who does not know."

"Mr. Galliard, must you continually throw your name in our faces? I am sure that, by this time, I know that you are one, Hippolyte Galliard, and I thank heaven for so much being clear to me; but it is all the rest of it that is beyond my understanding. You make it sound as though the Duke of Pevensey has, for some reason of his own, presented you to us as a gift."

"Exactement, madame!" exclaimed Galliard, overjoyed with Lady Pollworth's sagacity.

163

"But why should he do such a thing?" demanded Pamela.

Galliard's eyes opened wide and he threw out his hands as he shrugged. "If ze mam'selle do not know, zen 'ow can poor Galliard?"

"Mama, I am completely at a loss to explain this—"

"The thing is, my child, what are we supposed to do with him? I am sure that I do do not know."

"For as long as we have him, why do we not let him work for us? After all, he is precisely what we have needed in our kitchen. Why, with the duke's own chef, we should be quite the envy of Mecklenburg Square, and need not be ashamed to look where we pleased for our company. Oh, Mama, we must take advantage of this opportunity that has come to us, for whatever reason!"

"I have not the least objection, but how do we explain matters to your father, my love? You know how he dotes upon Mrs. Biggam's cookery."

"Pardon, madame, but zis no big trouble to Hip—mille pardons, madame—I do not say my name again," he grinned apologetically as he checked himself. "You 'ave not to worry 'bout ze monsieur. I, Hi—hee, hee!—I shall make such dishes as monsieur 'as nevair tasted before. He will adore!"

"Galliard, that is precisely the difficulty. His lordship has no taste for new dishes. He is more than content with the old fare, and that is why he will not consider giving Mrs. Biggam up. In fact, he has tasted of the French cuisine at his club and expressed vehement dissatisfaction with it."

"Pah! for ze club! Zey have not Galliard! I cook for monsieur and he adores! It is all! I go now to make ready in ze kitchen!"

He bowed, turned about and walked out of the room, putting his nose up as he passed by Gibbs.

Looking completely helpless, the butler inquired: "Madam?"

Lady Pollworth was frowning as she said: "Kindly inform Mrs. Biggam not to fret, and for the nonce, until we have disposed of that monstrous man, to stay clear of him."

"Very good, your ladyship."

As soon as he was gone, Lady Pollworth turned to Pamela: "If we are to credit his claims, then we are in an odd situation, indeed. Pamela, surely you must know something more than you have said. Why, I have not the least idea what wages he expects. Do you think I ought to make inquiry of her Grace?"

"Then you think we ought to keep him on?"

"I do not see that we have any choice. If the duke actually did send him on to us as some sort of gesture, and not just to be rid of the fellow, then we shall have to keep him until we have learned what his Grace meant by it."

"But there is Papa."

"Yes, there is Papa," sighed her ladyship. "And, furthermore, there is Mrs. Biggam, too. What ever are we to do with *her?*"

"We could send her back to Surrey," suggested Pamela.

"Oh, I should hate to have to listen to what your father would say to it! Then, too, we do not know for how long his Grace intended for this Galliard to cook for us. We should be in a pretty pickle if we had packed Mrs. Biggam off to the estate and his Grace demanded his chef back. Oh dear, why did you ever have to start up with him in the first place?

"But then there is a bright side to the business, isn't

there," she went on happily. "We can assume that we are on the friendliest terms with the Lyttons and, for as long as we have got this Galliard, we can entertain right royally."

Pamela smiled uncertainly. "I dare say, but it is a puzzle what is behind this kindness of his Grace—if it is a kindness at all."

"I am sure I do not know, child. Let your father deal with it. It is all his fault, you know. If he had consented to engage one of these French chefs in the first place, none of this ever would have occurred."

Lady Pollworth, distressed with the culinary calamity that had descended upon her domicile, required expert advice from sources, more mature than her daughter, to assist her in dealing with it. It was but a short walk to Lady Fairchild's, in whom she had faith, and she suggested that Pamela accompany her to the Fairchild's residence, saying, offhandedly: "It is possible that Kevin might be there, you know, and we have not seen him in ages, the dear boy."

But Pamela had other plans, more tempting than even the definite promise of seeing Kevin. She declined her mother's invitation and saw her ladyship off. Then she descended to the kitchen.

Chapter XIII

She was amazed by the scene that greeted her eyes. Galliard was standing in the center of the kitchen, shouting orders, punctuating each command with a shake of his "baton." He would use his spoon not only to point in the direction he demanded the slavey to go, but would menace the laggards with it as well. Not that any one appeared to be slow in obeying his instructions.

Oddly enough, a stern frown of disapproval on her face, Mrs. Biggam was standing to one side, her arms folded across her bosom, observing the frenetic activity that was taking place in her kitchen.

To Pamela, that last was a good sign. Perhaps, it would not be necessary to send Mrs. Biggam away. Now, if she could only arrange with Galliard for a reasonable repast to set before her father for his evening meal, things might be less-objectionable to his lordship so that some sort of reasonable debate might ensue.

That was her purpose in coming down to speak with the Frenchman. She feared that his high-handed methods would come a cropper before her father, if changes were made in his tablefare that were too sudden and too drastic. Since they had now got themselves a French chef, half the battle was won. It would be a shame to lose it all, after having come so far.

At the sight of her, Galliard, came over at once, his face all smiles.

"Ah, mam'selle, you 'ave come to speak wiz me. I am so ver' happy."

"Monsieur, I pray that you have not begun your preparations yet?"

"But of course, I 'ave! I would make the grande feast for monsieur!"

"Oh, but you must not! It would be better if you made something quite plain for his lordship. I do not think he will appreciate your efforts if they come upon his so suddenly."

"But ever' one adores ze efforts of Hippolyte Galliard! Ah, mam'selle, you do not mind if I speak my name, no? To me, it 'as ze sound of music!"

"No, I do not mind—but I was thinking that if you would make some English dish for his lordship—Mrs. Biggam, would you join us for a moment?"

From the look upon Mrs. Biggam's broad face, Pamela thought for a moment the woman was about to refuse to oblige her, but, as it was her place to obey, Mrs. Biggam unfolded her arms and drew near.

Pamela then went on to explain how she wished the evening's meal to be prepared. She pointed out that it had to be a proper English dish that was set before his lordship. Mrs. Biggam's face mirrored her delight at the news, and she directed a superior glance at Galliard. Galliard's face fell, his mustache bristled, and his lower lip was thrust out. He was looking decidedly mulish.

Pamela quickly went on to say how marvelous was the French cuisine, she had heard so much about it; but unfortunately neither she nor her family were all that familiar with it. Nonetheless, she was sure that many English dishes were quite superior in their own way, and it would not hurt Monsieur Galliard to learn from Mrs. Biggam.

Before the chef could explode into a verbal fusillade of outraged French, she pointed at him and declared how necessary it was for a self-respecting family to be able to offer a fine example of the cuisine française, which was all the rage in the highest circles of Society. This appeared to mollify the Frenchman somewhat.

"And what a marvelous opportunity for two such eminent practitioners of the culinary arts to learn from each other. I dare say, monsieur, that you have never tried English cookery as done by Mrs. Biggam, have you?"

Since he had but just become acquainted with the woman, Galliard was at a loss as to how to make the point that it would have been beneath his dignity to have made the attempt.

Pamela then proceeded to inform Mrs. Biggam how necessary she was to an English family, practically raised upon her tasty and wholesome cooking, and immediately repeated her thought as to the further necessity of staying up with the world with regard to the kitchen arts.

Mrs. Biggam was relieved to learn that she was not to be completely displaced by the foreigner and would continue to have her day in the Pollworth kitchen.

She was quite satisfied and her face showed her contentment.

Galliard was not happy. He looked frustrated. For a little bit, he appeared to be conducting a debate in French with himself, muttering Gallic incomprehensibilities to the air. Finally, he gave a great shrug.

Shaking his head sadly, he said: "Nevair 'ave I, Hippolyte Galliard, been so insult. Hélas, what can I do? Nossing. Le bon duc 'as say to me: 'Hippolyte, to la belle Mam'selle Pollworth you go—wiz compliments.' I go wiz compliments. For monseigneur le duc, I do zis thing. Mam'selle, Galliard, he hears; Galliard, he obeys."

Pamela was very proud of what she had accomplished in the kitchen as she went back upstairs.

It was evening, the dinner hour was approaching, and Lord Pollworth was up in his chambers, changing his attire for dinner. Lady Pollworth and Pamela were awaiting his descent, sitting together in the small chamber off the dining room.

Her ladyship was not as nervous she might have been, had not Pamela informed her of her progress with the kitchen staff. They both agreed that Mrs. Biggam's preparing the meal would put off a discussion of the new acquisition, but not for long. Galliard would have to be brought to Lord Pollworth's attention, some time after the meal was ended. It could hardly be postponed beyond that. At least they would have the meal in peace—not that either of them was very hungry.

Finally, his lordship came down, and they went into the dining room. The meal was served, and as the soup bowls were placed before them, Pamela's nose told her that all was not as well as she had hoped.

Somehow, the ordinary English meal had developed a fragrance which, although it was zesty, was new to her. She saw the shocked look upon her mother's face, and knew that the secret of Galliard's presence in the Pollworth's kitchen could remain a secret no longer. Both she and Lady Pollworth gazed anxiously in Lord Pollworth's direction.

His lordship was engrossed in relating a tale of his successes in the City that day, and was unaware that he was sniffing at the air. The latter act, must have been purely unconscious, because, without hesitation, he dipped his spoon into his bowl, and raised it to his lips.

Pamela could no longer look at her mother. Her attention was focused upon every move of her father's. She wondered if she ought to say something before the storm broke, but there appeared no sign of dissatisfaction as Lord Pollworth, a smile on his lips, dipped into his bowl again for another spoonful.

After the second taste, he stared down at the soup and exclaimed: "I say, what have we here? Mrs. Biggam has quite outdone herself, I perceive. But I do not understand it. This is muttonball soup, is it not? Here, see the balls of meat in it." He fished about in his bowl and came up with a small specimen.

Looking to his wife, he went on; "Correct me if I am mistaken, but this *is* muttonball soup."

There was a meekness in Lady Pollworth's voice as she replied: "Yes, it is—or at least I believe that it is. It certainly has all the appearance of muttonball soup."

"But have you tasted it? I say, have you tasted it, m' dear? It is quite different, a flavor something stronger, yet definitely more appealing—and you do know how much I fancy muttonball soup."

"Then you do like it, my lord?"

"I should be out of my skull if I do not. Pray, see that my compliments are forwarded to Mrs. Biggam. Tell her it is a dashedly good soup."

Pamela was hoping that her mother would take this moment to inform her father of the addition to their culinary staff. She was thinking there would never be a better time for it.

But all Lady Pollworth did, was to look relieved, and pick up her own spoon. Pamela could not sit back and let the good chance pass. She said: "Papa, I am very pleased that you find the fare good, for I believe that another hand helped prepare it. It is not all Mrs. Biggam's work, you see."

Lord Pollworth paused and stared at his daughter, his spoon stayed upon the threshold of his mouth. Slowly, he lowered it, still staring hard at his daughter.

"I see. You have disobeyed me. You thought to come it over me by getting you a Frenchman into this house after I had expressly forbidden it. Daughter, it is done, but _I_ am not finished. Whoever it is will be sent packing at once. As for you, you shall be sent to your room, where you will stay for a day or more, as I see fit, until you have come to an understanding of the word 'obedience.'

"Constance, did you know about this? I pray you did not. It would be a heart's wound to know that my own wife schemed and plotted behind my back—and what is far worse, encouraged my daughter, the apple of my eye to do the same."

"Frederick Pollworth, you are a fool! An utter fool! Of course, I have not schemed and plotted against you, nor has your daughter. Though, I must say, I should not have blamed her if she had."

Lord Pollworth was beginning to look very uncomfortable. His lady was rarely in a mood to withstand him, but when she did, he soon learned that he was speaking out of order, and would be embarrassed for the hastiness of his conclusions and the sharpness of his tongue. Seeing the look in her eye, he knew he had done it again and was in for a rough time.

"It so happens, my dear lord and master, that, while it is true we have gained us a French chef, it was neither through Pamela's fault nor my own. You owe the both of us an abject apology, and that is all I have to say on the subject."

She put her spoon firmly down upon the tablecloth and glared angrily at his lordship.

Lord Pollworth knew that now had come the worst part of the tiff. From her attitude, he could be sure he was in the wrong, and he could be just as sure that she was not about to explain wherein he had erred. He was going to have to plead with her for the explanation, the petitioning going on for a length of time in direct proportion to the seriousness of his offense. He suspected that he had outdone himself, and it would be nigh bedtime before he would have the straight of the matter.

Fortunately for him, a glance in his daughter's direction revealed that she was quite eager to defend her mother, and herself, and a canny look filled his eye.

He turned to Pamela and said: "Pamela, my sweet, if I have cause to offer apology to you and your dear mother, I should be only too happy to do so. But it would help me if I were to be informed as to how I came to offend."

"Oh, Papa, it was the duke's doing!" she exclaimed. "It was the most surprising thing!"

"The duke! Which duke?"

173

"The Duke of Pevensey, of course. He sent his chef to us with his compliments."

"Daughter, this no time for a jest!" he cautioned sternly. "If you are going to offer me an explanation, make it credible, I pray—but the Duke of Pevensey? I strain to understand what his connection with the business can be, and I fail."

"Yes, Frederick, the child speaks the truth. We have got us Monsieur Hippolyte Galliard, formerly his Grace's chef, and now ours. But do not press me for his Grace's reasons. I am sure I cannot fathom them."

"If you mean to say that the duke gave the fellow the sack, then do not beat about the bush. It changes nothing. I had forbidden you to hire any such person—"

"There you go, off on a tangent, Frederick. It is no use talking to you, you will not listen."

"My love, indeed I am trying to understand, but this is ridiculous!"

"Then his Grace is ridiculous, for that is exactly what has occurred. This Galliard, by his own statement, has come to us at his Grace's expressed wish."

"The devil you say! *I* say he has got his nerve!"

"But, Papa," interjected Pamela, "the poor man had no choice but to do as his master bid him."

"Pamela, I pray you will not interrupt your mother and myself when we are having a conversation."

Lady Pollworth drew herself up and declared: "My lord, *I* am not having a conversation! Furthermore, I am in complete agreement with our daughter. Our chef was but doing his master's biding."

"I was not referring to the blighter! I was referring to his master. What business is it of his Grace to send his chef to our house, I ask you? Does he think I am not capable of selecting my own servants? The fellow is going back to Bloomsbury Square, and on the instant!"

"Oh, but, Papa, you cannot do that!" protested Pamela. "It would be a slap to the Lyttons; his Grace, in particular. I do believe that he thought he was doing us a favor."

"Favor? Why, I hardly know the gentleman!"

"Then it is for my sake he did it," responded Pamela blushing.

"Eh?!" exclaimed Lord Pollworth.

"Pamela, you go too far!" cried Lady Pollworth.

"I assure you that it must be so. Mrs. Biggam and Monsieur Galliard were on the outs when I went down to them this afternoon, but as soon as I put my foot down with them, it was quite another story. Monsieur immediately agreed to try to work with Mrs. Biggam, and actually, I had more difficulty getting her to agree to work with him, than the other way round. It was only because it was the duke's wish, as Monsieur Galliard informed me."

"A likely tale!" scoffed his lordship.

"How very interesting!" exclaimed her ladyship.

"I think it is because I had informed his Grace of our lack of a decent cook that he did it," explained Pamela.

Lord Pollworth stared at his daughter, and then turned his gaze back on his wife.

Lady Pollworth was looking wide-eyed at him and shaking her head. "Can you believe this, Frederick?" she asked.

His lordship turned again to his daughter. "Pamela, are you certain of this?"

"It came up in a conversation that I had with him, Papa. I never thought he would take me so seriously— but surely, you can understand how gracious it was of

175

him, and how bad it would look if we were to send Monsieur Galliard back to him."

"Gracious is hardly the word." He placed both his hands upon the table and nodded very soberly. "Aye, I dare say the matter of the chef is settled. We shall just have to put up with him. The blasted foreigner is a gift from the duke—but, what in heaven's name does it portend? I mean to say, duke or no duke, a chap does not send his chef off to a friend as a gift. I can see it as a loan, but his Grace's action—Constance, I am baffled! What do you think of the matter?"

"Then it is all right? We can keep the chef?" cried Pamela.

"I do not see that we have any choice—and, besides, if the fellow can so quickly make changes in Mrs. Biggam's cookery and to such delicious effect, I, for one, shall go to the trouble of expressing my gratitude to his Grace—But, I am still not sure that I understand what moved him to do it."

"I am sure that it was a kind heart, Frederick," suggested Lady Pollworth.

"I am not so sure, my dear, and I think I shall have to look into the matter further. Pamela, my sweet, precisely what was it that you said to his Grace with regard to our cook?"

Pamela's cheeks turned red and she bit her lip. "I admit it was very childish of me, Papa, but I did mention the fact that we could not entertain properly for lack of a decent table, and that it would hurt my chances to meet eligible gentlemen when word of it got about."

Once again her parents exchanged glances.

"Oh, Papa, surely you do not think his Grace would have gone to such a length because of my silly remark. No, I suspect that it was more the result of Mrs.

Biggam's infatuation with rosewater. His Grace must have thought we suffered dreadfully with our cook, and sent his along, to ease our problem."

"Ah yes, every now and again Mrs. Biggam does overdo the rosewater. You know, Constance, I was meaning to speak to her on that subject. It could prove to be extremely embarrassing were we to have guests—"

"But, Frederick, pray whom do you think that the duke and duchess were if they were not our guests? It has already happened! I told you how mortified I was, and you passed it over lightly."

"Hmm, yes, I dare say, I should have spoken to her sooner. Ah well, it appears that the matter has been mended. What, with the duke's own chef in our kitchen, we shall be quite unexceptional. It certainly speaks well to the point with regard to how the Lyttons feel about us as neighbors and friends. The question is what is truly behind it. Rather a cheery prospect, don't you think?"

"Frederick Pollworth, at times you can be a most exasperating man!" exclaimed Lady Pollworth. "Had you only listened to me in the first place, and found a chef for us, none of this might have happened."

His lordship did not look at all perturbed. He smiled and replied: "Quite, my dear. You must admit it was a most fortunate stroke, as it happened."

A smile broke forth upon her ladyship's lips. "You are quite right, you know. Bears thinking on, doesn't it?"

Pamela was thoroughly confused by this time. She could not make head nor tail of their exchange. To her, it sounded as though they were blowing hot and cold at the same time.

"Mama, I am sure I do not understand what it is

that you and Papa are saying. Are we keeping Hippolyte or are we not?"

"Of course we are, pet," replied his lordship. "I would not think of parting with the good fellow. He is, practically, a gift from his Grace. Why what would the duke think of me?"

"But, Papa, it was just a moment ago that you were so incensed. What has brought on this change in you?"

Lord Pollworth cast a quizzical glance at his daughter. "Truly, I do not have to explain the obvious to you, my dear." He turned to his wife. "I say, Constance, can our daughter be such a slowtop? I mean to say, surely she, of all of us, must know what is going on."

"Pamela, dear child, your father and I are thrilled at the prospect of the Duke of Pevensey entertaining a *tendre* for you. You do see how *that* is, do you not?

"Oh, Mama, you cannot be serious! I have been in the duke's company but twice. He is handsome and he is wealthy and he is very likely the most charming gentleman I have ever spent any time with, but that is hardly any reason for Gerald to be interested in *me*. As for the chef, it is quite possible that the duke was not too satisfied with the cuisine—"

"Rubbish, my dear! You are speaking rubbish!" exclaimed Lord Pollworth. "Just taste what he has done with the muttonball soup! It is superb! Constance, whatever is that fresh taste he has managed to put into it?"

"A bit of anise, I think. Such a simple thing to make all that difference. Oh, I cannot wait for our first 'at home.' I am sure that none of our neighbors in the square have anything to compare. Pamela, you and I must sit down together and begin at once to send out invitations—"

"But what are we to do with Mrs. Biggam?" queried

Pamela. "I had a most difficult time to get her to agree to work with monsieur."

Lord Pollworth frowned. "It would be a shame to lose her services. But, I say—" and his face brightened —"what is there to say to our having two chief cooks in the kitchen, one for the good and hearty English dishes, and one for the fancy French ones? Stab me, but that would be something new in cookery, don't you think?"

"Why, Frederick, how very clever of you to think of it! Of course! I should be surprised if we were not to be the leaders in a new fashion of entertaining. We could have French nights to alternate with English nights— and what a coup it would be if, as with this muttonball soup, between our two cooks they managed to come up with an entirely new and novel cuisine! Oh, I am just too excited to speak! Pamela dear, let us repair to the kitchen at once, and discuss this with our two prizes."

"I beg your pardon, my lady, but I should prefer to continue with my repast. What is the use of our having chefs if we are not the first to benefit from their efforts?"

In the face of his lordship's disapproval, the ladies began to partake of the soup. The first spoonful and all three looked up and exclaimed: "It is cold!"

As Lord Pollworth was beginning to look annoyed, Lady Pollworth immediately had the bowls returned to the kitchen for reheating and ordered that the next remove be served.

Lord Pollworth smiled broadly and began to look with great anticipation towards the door where the next course would make its appearance.

Pamela, too, was feeling the stirrings of appetite, now that the great problem in her life was in a fair way to being solved.

Chapter XIV

The crisis was past and Pamela's spirits ascended to a level of happy enthusiasm. Now, the Pollworths could entertain the world and have naught to be ashamed of. Papa was going to keep Hippolyte on, and Mama was already busy with her interminable task of preparing guest-lists.

As a young lady of noble family, she had arrived at that age where it was now her business and delight to enter into Society and make what conquests she could. In her case, it was not all that new, for she had done quite well for herself in Surrey, where she had had all the advantages of breeding and wealth.

Here, in London, it was a little different. Mecklenburg Square boasted a noble family in almost every house, and without exception, each of the young ladies in the neighborhood had gentility and affluence to compare with her own. They each also had a French chef under their several roofs, and now, this great advantage was no longer theirs alone. Pamela could hold up her head and go forth to the various entertainments and affairs, knowing that the Pollworths were able to repay, in kind, their social obligations.

It was not an overwhelming joy that filled Pamela, but more a feeling of ease with her lot. What had been uncomfortable before was now unexceptional. She had become a member in good standing of the community, with the advent of Hippolyte Galliard into the Pollworth household.

With regard to the Duke of Pevensey, she was not so easy. She found it incredible that her parents should have seen so much in his Grace's gesture, yet she had to admit that another explanation for Gerald's generosity was not easy to find. If Hippolyte had been a poor sort of specimen as a chef, it might have gone off as a joke; but, as in the days that followed, he proved himself to be a superb master of the French cuisine, it could not be taken as any sort of jest.

Yet, to think about Gerald as being warmly interested in the Pollworths, namely, herself, brought on such an intense emotion within her as to make her blush. If he had not been a duke, and therefore so far above her, she must certainly have set her cap for him. It was a thought echoed by all her friends as they, too, puzzled over the meaning that lay behind his Grace's conduct. Pamela had grave doubts of having meetings with his Grace until she was more assured of his intent.

Was there something special, some particular message, in it for her? Or was it just the act of a very rich gentleman, a kindness performed on the spur of the moment, with no meaning to it at all? She never doubted but that his Grace had found a replacement for Hippolyte in short order, and she could even imagine his annoyance at having to go to that trouble.

No, her parents could not have been right. The Duke of Pevensey was not possibly be interested in her that way. Just to prove herself correct on that point, she would wait and see if he made any further advance in her direction. Not that she expected him to, you understand—but, oh, how she wished he would!

The fangs of the ferocious winter were drawn, and as spring came to bless the land, Paris fell to the allies. The celebration over Napoleon's defeat added luster and joy to the social season just commencing.

Lord Pollworth had kept his vigil well. The family's fortune was in a way to being multiplied, and his constant presence in the City was no longer required. As far as he was concerned, if his family wished to return to Surrey, he would not object.

But the distaff side of the family most certainly *would* object to leaving the city. It was never a question with regard to Geoffrey. He was well begun on a promising career in politics with his new secretaryship. No one even thought to consult him in the matter. But, as far as Lady Pollworth and daughter were concerned, it was not to be contemplated.

Her ladyship had finally managed to put together a guest-list, after the most excruciating efforts, and Pamela had every wish to take advantage of the forthcoming Season. Now that the family had got a chef that they could be proud of, she insisted that they show him off—and themselves as well, of course. The winter had been a miserable one and she had had no chance at all to see London. It would be most unfair to her if they were now to depart, and the season just beginning. Furthermore, whatever would they do with Hippolyte in Surrey?

Lord Pollworth, in the face of the female insurrection, hastily pointed out that it was just a suggestion, and that he, for one, would be quite happy to stay on. He had no intention of giving up the house in any case, and he quite agreed that a taste of city Society would be good for all of them.

With the guest-list settled, and the weather, too, Lady Pollworth was almost ready to appoint the days for the Pollworth dinner parties; but it had become apparent to her and Pamela that neither of them had anything fitting to wear. The clothes they had brought with them from Surrey were hoplessly out of fashion. Before they did another thing, they must visit the shops.

Lord Pollworth was no great hand for formal entertaining, and anything that would postpone the ordeal was welcome to him. He knew how long it would take for his wife and daughter to properly outfit themselves, and he gave them every encouragement. He had no pressing matters to attend to, and was quite content to take his ease at his home, or at his club. In fact, he had quite a bit to say with regard to the old-fashioned table that was set before the membership, and moved, at the next meeting, that a proper French chef be engaged, never failing to refer to his own good fortune in that regard.

Pamela and Lady Pollworth went off to Pall Mall, to the firm of Harding, Howell & Co., situate in Schomberg House, where they not only could find anything they wished, but it was all of the finest quality, its goods and wares being designed for a most exclusive trade.

It was a huge and impressive establishment, even for London. There was no other like it in the city, much less the rest of the country. Haberdashery of every description, furniture, perfumes, ornamental items—why, a part of one floor was even devoted to a restaurant! And the staff! All of forty persons were employed on the premises in making up the various articles for sale, and in attendance on the different departments!

Needless to say, it took all of their first visit for the ladies to comprehend the possibilities of the place, and on their subsequent visits, who could blame them if they managed to purchase a deal more than just apparel?

Lord Pollworth tried. He pointed out that they were supposed to be shopping for their spring attire, not to refurbish the house. He was not made of money, you know.

Lady Pollworth regarded him for a moment with disdain, and then inquired: "Are our fortunes in such a sad state? It was but a few days ago you claimed that we had naught to worry about, my lord."

"So I did, but that does not go to say that we have to spend every penny of it!"

"I am sure that we are not about to. We are merely purchasing a few things that are badly needed. You would not wish for your daughter to appear in anything but the best light, would you?"

"Of course, I do not, but—"

"Then you must remember that our house, as it is the setting in which she shall be entertaining our guests, is every bit as important as her apparel. I do not intend to spare a shilling in her benefit."

"Fiddlesticks! We needed no such jiggumbobs and jimcracks in Surrey!"

"Then, my lord, in the event you have not yet noticed it, we are living in London and not in Surrey—and I can assure you that what was good enough for the shires will never do for the city. Pamela must have the best of everything. Do you think that the other gentlemen in the square are stinting their daughters? I should say not! Pamela in no orphan-child, and I intend that the world shall make a thorough note of it!"

"Now, Constance, there is no need to shout "

"Frederick, I am very exercised at the moment. Why, when I think of all the fuss you raised about our cooks, only to find that you *did* appreciate the French food when it was properly prepared—"

"Ah, yes, I was sure I had not heard the last of *that!* Very well, my lady, do as you see fit. It is not worth my peace to continue this profitless debate."

He stalked out with great dignity.

The ladies decided it was the better part of wisdom to henceforth restrict their shopping activities to the dress and millinery departments of Harding, Howell & Co.

Lady Pollworth and Pamela stepped out into the warm sunshine flooding Pall Mall, and paused to look about them. Behind them, their two footmen came to a stand, their arms filled with packages, while they awaited instructions from their mistress.

"It is a lovely day," said Lady Pollworth. "I should like to walk about for a bit, before we depart for home."

She was not looking at Pamela as she spoke, and, therefore, grew impatient when her daughter failed to respond. She had to repeat herself.

"Pamela, where are you?" she exclaimed as she turned to find her daughter looking off into the distance. "Pamela, you are not listening!"

At this point, Pamela turned to her mother and cried: "Mama, is not that the carriage of the Duke of Pevensey?"

"If it is, then your eyes are a deal sharper than your ears! Pamela, I was speaking to you. I said—"

"Yes, yes, Mama! I did hear you, but if that is his Grace in the carriage, perhaps he is coming this way!"

"In that case, it would be only neighborly for us to greet him, I am sure." Her ladyship then instructed the patient footmen to retire to the carriage with the parcels.

Turning back to Pamela, she surveyed her with critical eyes. Quite satisfied with her daughter's appearance, she asked: "How do I look? It would be just like a man to come upon one when one is not at one's best. Shopping is such a tedious labor." She primped at her hair, straightened her bonnet, and had just donned a smile of welcome when the carriage drew to a halt before them.

The Duke of Pevensey stepped down and came over to them with a cheery greeting.

"Ah, the lovely Pollworth ladies! I had intended to call upon you, but her Grace is suffering from a slight indisposition—"

"Oh, I do hope it is nothing serious, your Grace. Have you had the doctor in?"

"Nothing so bad as that, Lady Pollworth. In fact, she seemed quite her old self, this morning. Thank you for your concern. But tell me, pray, how goes it with Hippolyte? I am dying to know if he has come up to your expectations."

Pamela was quite content to leave the burden of the conversation to her mother and stood quietly by. She was aware that the duke was casting glances at her. In fact, she surmised that his last question was directed more to her than to her mother.

Lady Pollworth responded, glibly: "Oh, your Grace, need you ask? The fellow is marvelous, and I wonder that you could even think to give him up."

He laughed. "I marvel myself that I did, but it was for a young lady in great distress, you see. Miss Pamela, you do not say a word. Has not Hippolyte permitted you to put your plans forward a little?"

Pamela knew very well to what he was referring, and her blush betrayed her thinking. There was a bantering look in his eye, and it was a cause of discomfort to her. She wished that they had never met.

She managed a smile and replied: "Thank you, your Grace, for your kindness. Monsieur Galliard has proven to be precisely what I wished."

"Then you do not see any further obstacle to your forthcoming marriage, I presume?"

"Marriage!" exclaimed Lady Pollworth. "Pamela, what is this strange implication of his Grace's?"

"It is purely nonsense, Mama. His Grace is making fun of me," replied Pamela, unhappily.

The duke's face fell, and he hurried to make amends: "Oh, my dear Miss Pamela, such was the farthest thing from my mind! I would never think of making fun of you. Were you not at all serious about the need of a chef to further your social ambitions?"

"Now you are making me out to be a climber!"

His Grace chuckled. "I seem to be putting my foot into it, deeper and deeper. Of course, I am perfectly serious. I thought that I was doing you a favor by sending Hippolyte to you."

"I do declare, your Grace, Lord Pollworth and my-self have been up nights pondering over the reason for your unlooked for generosity," Lady Pollworth broke in. "Pamela, I wish you would inform your mother what this is all about. And, your Grace, I must say that I am no end puzzled about the busi-ness. There was no explanation along with Galliard, you know."

"If I have caused you and Pamela the least bit of uneasiness, Lady Pollworth, I am devastated, but I thought that Miss Pamela understood, and that there was no need for an explanation. I say, Pamela, you do recall our conversation with regard to chefs, do you not?"

"Indeed, your Grace, and I am embarrassed beyond words that you should have taken my silly remarks so seriously—"

"Then you are not pleased with Hippolyte, and there-fore, not with me either."

"Oh, but on the contrary, your Grace! Hippolyte was precisely what was needed—"

"Pamela, I do not think I am beginning to care for this conversation," exclaimed Lady Pollworth. "If it is making any sense at all to me, I gather that you petitioned his Grace to assist you to what? Marriage? With whom, may I ask? Nor am I particularly clear in my mind, at this moment, what Monsieur Galliard has to do with anything at all, except the Pollworth kitchen!"

Pamela racked her brain for a response that would ease the embarrassment of the present situation. She could see the light of amusement in his Grace's eyes. It did nothing to lessen the burning of her cheeks.

But Lady Pollworth, too, was aware of the awkwardness of the conversation, and had every wish to bring it to an end.

"Your Grace, I have the feeling that something exceptional has taken place between Pamela and you, something of which I am sure I do not wish to hear another syllable. I offer my apology, and that of my daughter, and wish to assure you that there shall be no repetition—in fact, as of this moment, my embarrassment is so great I am seriously considering removing the family back to Surrey—as a matter of fact, it was only the other day that Lord Pollworth and I were discussing that very possibility. Of course, I would have none of it, but if I had but known how my daughter had implored—begged even—"

"Oh, Mama, it was nothing like that at all! Gerald, I pray you will inform my lady mother precisely how it went, or I shall never hear the end of it! And I do not think it is a bit funny!!"

At that, the duke burst into delighted laughter, while the two ladies stared at him in frank indignation.

"A thousand pardons, my ladies! I could not help it! You can not know how remarkable the business has become—but let me assure you, Lady Pollworth, Pamela never begged anything of me. I sent Hippolyte to you, only because it was my pleasure to do so. I understood from Pamela the difficulties you faced, to provide a fitting table for your company, and like any good neighbor, took the opportunity to be of assistance. I gather that you find Hippolyte to your taste and so I am happy with the result. Now then, if I can carry you ladies to wherever you are bound, you have but to command me. It will be my sincere pleasure to accommodate you."

As mother and daughter had had more than enough

of the duke's sense of whimsy, it took no effort upon their part to assure him that it was not at all necessary he put himself to the trouble. They had their own carriage, and were even, at that moment, on the point of returning to it.

Chapter XV

Pamela was not surprised. She had not been looking forward to another meeting with the duke, and now she understood the reason for it. She had done a silly thing, and his Grace was enough of a boor to have carried the business beyond good taste. She did not care if they never met again.

Unfortunately, she was not sure that there was any way to prevent their paths from crossing in the future. She was bound to meet him at an affair given by some neighbor or mutual acquaintance. Her friends chattered on about all the wonderful people their parents were planning to entertain, and the Lyttons were always high up on their lists. Even her own mother made no secret of her intention of inviting the duke and duchess.

Pamela, rather dispiritedly, attempted to persuade her mother that the duke was too high in the instep for them, but she quickly retreated in the face of her mother's indignation.

"Pamela, of late I am finding it ever more difficult to understand you! After what his Grace has done for us, I should think that he must be the very first to be invited. What ingratitude! In any case, everyone I know is planning to invite him, and we should look rather queer if we were the only family to ignore him. Now let us speak upon something more sensible!"

Thus Pamela was put to the discomfort of deciding how she would greet his Grace when next she saw him. It would not be easy. If he maintained that air of amusement with her, she was sure she would give him short shrift. But he was a duke and one had to step carefully with such eminence. Perhaps, if she made believe not to see his smile and the way the corners of his eyes crinkled with merriment as he inquired after Hippolyte, it would not be so bad.

Over the next few days, she reviewed how it might go, what he would say to her, and what she would say to him, constantly revising the exchange as though it were a little play, and she, the playwright.

She experienced some trouble with her reckonings, because the more she worked at it, the more it became evident to her that he would never take seriously her rejoinders. He was so superior in his odd humor to be her benefactor that she must always be at a disadvantage with him. If only there were some way to return Hippolyte to him, the situation for her might be improved.

But, alas, that was impossible. Neither her father nor her mother would allow it. Her mother was quite pleased to have Monsieur Galliard in her kitchen, and Lord Pollworth was become quite the gourmet, forever praising to the skies the various dishes that appeared before him. Less and less of Mrs. Biggam's taste and touch were evident in them, so that the Pollworths were sitting down, every evening, to dinners fit for a duke.

Despite her own difficulties, Pamela, too, was not anxious to lose the services of Hippolyte, either. As long as he was in the Pollworths' service, she had no qualms about the appearance she and her family would make even if royalty were to be included amongst their guests.

Still, despite her annoyance with the duke, Pamela had so much to look forward to, she was able to relegate his Grace to a far corner of her thoughts, and devote herself to the Season, which was then beginning. She was thoroughly prepared to show herself off to the world. Her wardrobe was filled with fine things, her parents were able to maintain an easy and affluential style, and best of all, they had Hippolyte Galliard to serve up dinners that every one must envy, even while they enjoyed them.

It was the Fairchilds who managed to open the Season in Bloomsbury. It was to be a dinner party, and the guest list was selected to include the most notable people in their acquaintance; but, as those few social nonpareils would hardly make for a large party, and as there had to be a fair crowd of others to impress, their neighbors in Mecklenburg Square were included, to fill out the roster. Naturally, the Lyttons were to be their most distinguished guests.

Eleanor Fairchild was very happy to announce to her friends the good news, and in all the detail that any one could have wished. Pamela, along with the rest, was interested to know, from the smallest party favor to the number of covers and removes, how the

Fairchilds planned to entertain and refresh their guests. Of course, the invitation list was subjected to the greatest scrutiny, too. Each of the young ladies was eager to learn all she could, so that she might report the facts to her mother, with an eye to making *her* family's affair even superior in some way that the Fairchilds had not thought of.

But, for Pamela, there was the further consideration of how she was to comport herself before his Grace, if he elected to attend. Not for anything would she consider feigning some excuse to be absent from the party; but, on the other hand, she was in some distress as to how to avoid being embarrassed by his Grace. One small consolation was the fact that, considering his attitude towards her, she need not expect him to ask her to dance with him. On further reflection, she did not see that as much of a consolation at all.

James Burton, the speculator responsible for developing much of Bloomsbury, and all of Mecklenburg Square, had leased out the sites to other builders; but, despite the different artisans to work on the structures, they all managed to present a similar appearance, both inside and outside. Thus, if one were familiar with one home in the square, one would be surprised only to the extent that any other resembled the first. Despite all the party decorations that might have disguised the rooms, Pamela found herself very much at home in their house.

Lady Pollworth, as usual, had the greatest difficulty in getting herself together for this particular event, whereas Lord Pollworth, for once, was prompt. Fortunately, for his temper, Geoffrey had arrived to accompany them, and his lordship was able to while away the time, of waiting for his lady, with inquiries as to how his son was getting along in his post. The net result was that the Pollworths were the last to arrive at the Fairchilds', even though they lived but a few doors away.

Lady Fairchild had just about concluded that her neighbors had been unavoidably detained, and the entire party was in the midst of entering the dining room, when the Pollworths arrived. Etiquette had to give way to the demands of a sumptous feast about to be served, so that Lady Fairchild hurried through the introductions with a poor grace, and, without a pause, went on with the seating of her guests.

For Pamela, it was a respite. All that there had been time for was a smile and a nod from the Lyttons, and she did not dare to raise her head long enough, before the duke, to determine the quality of his manner towards her.

Since he was seated in the place of honor at her host's right hand, and she was seated down near the foot of the table, with the other young people, she did not have to enter into conversation with him. But she was uncomfortably aware that his gaze wandered down to her rather often, and she found herself unable to refrain from returning the compliment. Since, more often than not, their eyes met, and his Grace smiled at her, it was only proper for her to smile back at him, so she told herself—as she tried to disguise from her own consciousness, an elevation of her pulse, that accompanied each little exchange.

The meal proved to be a good one. It was French of course, and Pamela enjoyed it, although she ate sparingly of the dishes, as did all the females. In the privacy of their own dining rooms, ladies might indulge themselves, but it was not the thing to do, when dining out. But, for all that the repast was well prepared and nicely seasoned, she believed that Hippolyte could have done better with it.

It was a desultory sort of chatter that proceeded along with the meal amongst the young ladies at table. They were well acquainted with each other, and were in each other's homes almost every day. Whatever new topics were to come into their ken would be found at this affair, overheard from the conversations of their elders, that were proceeding farther up on the table. It was a strain upon their ears and minds to listen to everything, while they maintained the pretense of chatting amongst themselves.

At the same time, they were very interested in the guest of honor. Every now and then, one of the young ladies, in the most innocent fashion, would let her eyes wander aimlessly about the table, taking careful note of whatever his Grace might be doing. Therefore, by the time the meal had progressed beyond the third remove, each young lady had formed a conclusion, that filled her with envy. Something was going on between the duke and their friend, Pamela.

That the Duke of Pevensey had sent his personal chef to serve the Pollworths was now common knowledge, and it had been a puzzle amongst the young ladies—and their parents, too—that Pamela gave the appearance of no great joy over the event. The exchange of glances, that was now going on under their very noses, was bound to incite their curiosity, to the degree that they wished they could get Pamela alone and ply her with questions.

Pamela was not insensitive to the affect his Grace's behavior was having upon her companions, and was wise enough to comprehend how their thoughts were making a confusion of any attempt at reasonable table talk. She did all in her power to make up for the lack, but was hard put to concentrate with any great effect. His Grace, despite his being at the far end of the room, was having a most devastating effect upon all the young ladies present, for one reason or another.

Pamela was exhausted by the time the meal ended. She was happy to retire with the ladies to the drawing room, leaving the gentlemen to their port and their tobacco.

But what had been an uncomfortable posture at the table, in the drawing room was transformed into an ordeal. More ladies than her young friends, made her the center of their attention, questions, and remarks. Some of the mothers joined in what rapidly became an interview rather than a conversation. Pamela, her cheeks flushed, found herself incapable of saying a word that was not taken for a sly inference by her audience. As a result, the rumors began to flourish, and they spread quickly about the great chamber.

Lady Pollworth had not been so observant at dinner, and so she was caught by surprise as the gossip began to swirl about her. Since, from the start, she had difficulty understanding what had given rise to these strange and impertinent questions from her neighbors, her answers fed the gossip, rather than quenched it. Soon, she too was surrounded by a group of dames, all intent upon determining in exactly what state was the Duke of Pevensey's affections.

Because she was easily the most formidable personage present in the drawing room, no one dared to approach her Grace for a clarification of the rumors, until the Honorable Henrietta Blandish, a most resolute young lady, driven beyond endurance, decided that the duke's mother must be the best person to confirm or deny what everyone was saying: his Grace had a tendre for Pamela Pollworth!

"Your Grace, by your leave, but it is being said that your son the duke and Miss Pollworth are of a mind to plight their troth with each other."

The dowager was not used to being addressed by young persons so informally, and her countenance immediately registered her disapproval. But Henrietta was not one to be easily cowed and she stood her ground, waiting.

On the other hand, her Grace had been filled with curiosity over all the excited buzzing that filled the room, and had an urgent wish to share in it, too.

She replied, as though from a very great height: "So that is what is being said, is it? Pray summon Miss Pollworth to me. I would speak with her."

It was a wish that Henrietta could not ignore. She hurried over to Pamela and extracted her from the little mob that was pressing her. Waving everyone away, she explained to Pamela her Grace's wish to speak with her.

Pamela's relief at being rescued from her friends was cut short. The Lady Charlotte was even less attractive to her at that moment than was the duke. There was reluctance in every line of her body as she made her way to the duchess, accompanied by an eager Henrietta.

To the latter's desappointment, she was thanked and dismissed. All she heard was her Grace bidding: "Pamela, dear child, do draw closer."

A nod from her Grace, and the few ladies, who had been sitting with her, arose, curtsied, and withdrew. The duchess motioned to Pamela to be seated and said: "Young lady, the most shocking tidings have but recently come to my ears, shocking because I believe them to be quite untrue. I demand to know why you are spreading them. Now, I do not state categorically that they are untrue, I merely believe it to be so, for I have not been informed by my son that there is any interest between the two of you. But, as I am only his mother, if it were up to him, I should be the last to be informed. I pray you, Miss Pamela, to inform me, herewith, precisely what *is* between the two of you."

Pamela was taken quite by surprise. The dowager's tone was not what she had been expecting. She had been preparing herself for a denunciation; at the very least, a challenge. Her Grace's manner was something more soft. Her request was not a demand, but a plea, and Pamela had to think a bit to determine how to answer her.

"Now, child, if you are preparing a falsehood for me, I pray you will not put yourself to the trouble. I put no obstacles in my son's path when he decided to send Galliard to you—you do know that he sent Galliard to *you,* did you not?" asked her Grace, puzzled by Pamela's blank look.

"No, your Grace, I did not. It was for my family's sake, I thought."

Her Grace laughed at her. "My, but you are not very bright. Poor Gerald, his grandiose gesture gone completely to waste—Oh, but surely, you must have known! The word is all about us, about Gerald and you!"

"I beg your pardon, your Grace, but I have heard what is being said. Though I deny any knowledge of the business, I am not believed. Are you *sure* that Gerald did this thing for *my* sake?"

Now it was the duchess's turn to be puzzled. She was suddenly very ill-at-ease. "Really, how can I be sure of anything!" she snapped. "Every thing is news to me! If you are not aware of what is going on, and you are the one who is concerned in it, who does?"

She frowned. "May I inquire how you come to address my son by his Christian name, then?"

"Did I do that? I beg your pardon, your Grace, I—I was not aware that I had."

Her Grace looked plainly dissatisfied with Pamela. "This conversation is not getting us anywhere at all. Have you been seeing my son on the sly, miss?"

"I most certainly have not, your Grace! I am quite sure that that is the last thing your son would wish!"

"Then, how do you explain Galliard?"

"I was under the impression that his Grace found the gesture excruciatingly comical," rejoined Pamela bitterly.

Again the duchess frowned. "No. No, that is not like my Gerald. I cannot believe that of him—ah, but here comes the miscreant now! I shall have the truth from him if I live!"

There was panic in Pamela as she turned to catch a glimpse of the gentlemen coming in to join the ladies. She saw his Grace, all smiles as usual, slowly making his way towards them. He was stopping to greet various people and to exchange a few words.

Pamela rose to leave.

"No, you must stay by me until this business is resolved," commanded her Grace. "See! He is being told something!"

Pamela could not resist looking over her shoulder once again.

His Grace was still smiling, but it was a different smile. She could see that old mocking laughter in his eyes, even at this distance. It was to begin again, the embarrassment, and this time before his mother. How could anyone in their right senses not see how cruel he could be?

"Ah, your Grace, it is rare that I find you enjoying such charming and beautiful company! Pamela, I am so pleased to see you. As a matter of fact I have a most important message for you. It is from one of your most devoted admirers."

Pamela turned a helpless glance to her Grace, who had a look of impatience on her face.

"Surely, Pamela, you have so many admirers you cannot guess from whom I come as message-bearer," said his Grace banteringly.

It was too much for the duchess. "Your Grace, it is not becoming in you to act the tease."

Pamela found that she could not take her eyes off his face. At the same time she was aware that the entire roomful of people were casting quizzical glances in their direction. All she could think of was what explanation she could give to her parents and her friends.

"Your Grace," firmly replied the duke, drawing himself up into an attitude of mock indignation. It was the twinkle in his eye that gave his pose away. "I beg to inform you I am *not* a tease. I have a perfectly valid message to deliver to Pamela, and if you will refrain from interfering, I shall proceed to do so at once."

The duchess, suppressing a smile, waved a derogatory hand at him. "Oh, do get on with your nonsense, Gerald! I can see that you are in one of your devilishly charming moods, and there is no doing anything with you, until you have done."

"Thank you, your Grace. You are kindness itself—considering how much you have put up with from me, your devoted son."

Her Grace chuckled and sat back with a shake of her head.

The duke turned his attention on Pamela and said: "I say, do you recall a tad, but once removed from an urchin, one very young person by name, Bertie?"

Pamela smiled. "Oh, but yes! How is the darling little fellow? I do hope that he has not fallen into too many scrapes in your service, your Grace."

There was a grimace on the duke's face as he turned to his mother and asked: "Mama, as you are a veritable fount of wisdom upon the matter of etiquette, may not this dear child address me as 'Gerald,' if I speak to her as 'Pamela'?"

"Gerald, as far as I am concerned, she can address you in any way that suits her—and the less complimentary the better, you rogue!"

She was truly enjoying herself as she turned to Pamela and said: "I pray you will humor his Grace, or we shall be here all evening before we ever learn about this marvelous message he was commissioned to deliver to you, my dear."

Pamela chuckled and replied: "Very well, Gerald, what is the message?"

"I say, would either of you ladies object if I sat myself down?" was his response. The duchess burst out laughing, and Pamela could not refrain from joining her.

Smiling broadly, the duke sat down and said: "Bertie took me aside this morning—he is very condescending with dukes, you see—and requested that I make clear to the kin' lydy if she be in the way of needing a pyge, 'e'd be bloody well erbliged—I beg your pardon, ladies, but I am trying to deliver it in the exact manner in which it was expressed—she'd 'member ol' Bertie. There, I think that was the way of it."

Pamela looked askance at his Grace. "Can it be that you are not treating the little fellow well, Gerald?"

"That is hardly to the point. The question ought to have been put: Is Bertie treating *me* well? That is, if you have any consideration for me."

Pamela laughed and replied: "Please tell Bertie for me, if ever I do find myself in need of a page, I shall most certainly 'member him."

"Then I must press you to find the need, fairly soon. Give Bertie two or three years, and he will make a monstrous big page, I am thinking. The way he puts his food away, he must grow great just to contain it all."

"Heavens! I should hire him right away if you would allow it, but I do not think my father would approve."

"If not your father, perhaps your husband. You do expect to be getting married shortly, or did I misunderstand you?"

Now her Grace was entranced with the conversation. Some people approached to address her, but she waved them away, impatiently.

Pamela blushed. "Oh, Gerald, you are not going on about the chef again, are you?"

"I only wish to hear that Hippolyte has made your pathway to matrimony easier. There was the difficulty of getting about to meet eligible gentlemen, you did say?"

"Of course, we are in a good way to entertain properly, if that is what *you* are getting at."

"That is precisely what I am getting at. It would seem, then, that the Lyttons, who are in a way your benefactors, are not to share in the benefits of their most gracious bequest. I have not seen any invitation from the Pollworths to me. Have you?"

"But your Grace, the Season is just starting! I can

assure you that my lady mother has many plans afoot, and that you and her Grace must be at the head of our very first list of guests."

He nodded perfunctorily and replied: "Then, indeed, I am gratified to learn that we have not been forgotten. I shall be looking forward to the Pollworths' first affair."

With that, he bowed slightly and walked off. Her Grace blinked thoughtfully after him, while Pamela frowned, quite confused at his abrupt change of manner.

Chapter XVI

A few weeks passed and the season was in full swing, but still the Pollworths had not seen fit to send out invitations. Pamela was growing very impatient with her mother. If it had been up to herself, the very day after the Fairchilds' party, the Pollworth invitations would have been sent out. She wanted very much to have her own party, so that she might have her chance at being the center of attraction, just as each of her friends, during the parties that their respective families sponsored.

She was not being cut, or otherwise ignored, at these affairs, but she felt herself under a cloud, as long as she could not return the hospitality. She felt, further, that despite her dance card always being filled she was not getting the attention she wished. It was all Gerald's fault, too.

His manner to her was faultless, up to a point. He

never failed to greet her, and there was always some small exchange between them. Very often, it was some odd little message from her devoted admirer, Bertie, enough for Gerald and she to enjoy a chuckle together. But that was where it ended. Gerald went on to dance with almost every female present; the almost, being herself.

The fact that he had not been invited to the Pollworths' must have had something to do with it. He managed, each time they spoke, to inquire how the invitations were coming. She wished she could have given him some definite word, but it was not in her power to do so. The invitation list of Lady Pollworth was undergoing revision after revision.

As her ladyship took great pains to explain to any one who inquired, she was having the greatest difficulty with her planning for the simple reason that there were just too many parties to attend. By the time she finished a list of guests, there would be another party, at which she would meet many new people, some of them quite worthy of being counted amongst her friends. Now, how would they feel if they were not included in the Pollworths' event? Naturally, quite poorly; so it was necessary to revise the list, and if one revised the list, one must revise the number of covers.

Then, it followed that one must consult with one's cook, and it invariably developed that an entirely new menu was needed. Truly, she did now know where she gained the strength to persist in this arduous duty! But she had, and it would not be any time at all before she would be able to issue invitations.

Pamela was beside herself with embarrassment over her mother's inability to respond to the awful situation that was developing. Every time she attended a ball, or other festivity, she found herself hoping that Gerald would be absent. As a duke, one would have thought that, after a while, with all the greater social events that were open to him, he would have found these neighborhood assemblies something of a bore, but it proved not to be the case. He was always there, and he was always the highest ranking guest. Pamela began to feel conspicuous, the only female that his Grace assiduously avoided dancing with, and even more so, when he made a point of coming over to hold his little conversations.

It sounded foolish in her own ears to have to place the blame for his not having received an invitation from the Pollworths upon her mother.

But there was something else that began to make itself felt. During all this time, she was in great demand by the other young gentlemen of the neighborhood, and could count herself a very popular young lady. At one time, it had been her greatest wish to achieve that eminence. In fact, it was precisely that desire, which had driven her to try to capture Hippolyte from out of his Grace's service.

The odd thing of it was that Hippolyte had still to prepare his first meal for the Pollworths' company, and here she was one of the most popular of her friends. It must have been obvious to a simpleton that a French chef was not at all requisite for making a good appearance.

And that was how she felt, a veritable simpleton. She had gone to great fuss, embroiled herself in a great embarrassment, to gain her end, and it had not been necessary at all. In fact, it appeared to be working against that which she truly desired, and had not realized, before she went and made such a goose of herself.

True, it was Hippolyte's presence in her family's kitchen that supported the pretension of a friendship with Gerald; but, by the same token, Gerald appeared to be using the chef as an excuse not to dance with her. He expected an invitation to share the delights of his former chef's cookery and was practically saying as much.

Oh, if only her mother would just make up her mind to go along with *any* list, so that Gerald would no longer have this odd pretext for not dancing with her! She knew that she wanted very much to be closer to him than she was. She would have liked to have had him chat with her, as in the past, and was filled with envy to see him laughing together with the other young ladies. While her mind was occupied with the unfairness of the situation, she still managed to engage the attention of the other gentlemen, but could not refrain from observing Gerald throughout the evening.

As it became very clear that Lady Pollworth would never accomplish her task, Pamela, out of her desperation, suggested that they forget the party, and just invite the Lyttons for an informal dinner.

Lady Pollworth, her face filled with shock, exclaimed: "Pamela, have you gone quite mad? Of course, we cannot do that! An informal dinner with the Duke of Pevensey? Can you begin to believe that the duchess would allow us to condescend to her? I should think not! The very idea! Child, this is not the first time you have suggested it, and I know that I am safe in saying it will not be the last; but appearances must be maintained. We have got to have a formal dinner, and we have got to have our friends to join us. Why, what a waste it would be if we just entertained their Graces by ourselves, and there was no one else to see!

"In any case, it is not to be thought of, at all. Everyone in the neighborhood has had an occasion to invite the entire neighborhood, and we should look awfully odd if we did not do as much."

"Mama, I do not say that we needs must never have our party. It is only that we owe a debt of gratitude to his Grace. What better way than to have him and the duchess sit down to a superb dinner prepared by Hippolyte? If you think about it, it would be something more than any of our neighbors could boast."

Lady Pollworth's face brightened. "Yes, that is a thought, my dear. And I must say, it would be a deal easier to prepare a dinner for just the Lyttons, than for the entire neighborhood. I mean to say, I shall not have to be at adding names to the guest-list, forever, if it were to be just for them, would I?"

"Quite, Mama. It would be ever so much easier, I am sure."

Now her ladyship was smiling, and there was great relief in her voice as she remarked: "Pamela, you have taken a huge load off my mind. That was a very intelligent suggestion. Let us go down and speak to Galliard at once."

Although the forthcoming entertainment was bound to cause Pamela qualms, she never had the chance to worry about the matter. Thanks to Lady Pollworth, she was kept very busy, right up to the fateful evening.

When her ladyship sat herself down to pen the invitations to the duke and duchess, it struck her that Lady Fairchild was such an excellent friend, it would be a shame not to include her. Then, as she penned the invitations for the Fairchilds, she became sure that, as long as she was writing, she might as well

211

add the Blandishes, and for the same reasons. The process did not stop with the Blandishes, either.

By the time she had done, the invitations, piled high upon her writing table, comprised a most formidable guest-list, something larger than any previous hostess in the neighborhood had devised. The reason was, of course, that the circle had grown immensely. At each affair, there had been new people added. By this time, the Pollworths' acquaintanceship had grown, although no greater than that of any other of the neighboring families, far beyond the bounds of Mecklenburg Square. Now, with the Pollworths' party coming at the end of the developing circle, Lady Pollworth could invite many more people than the preceeding hostesses had been able to. Considering her approach to the matter, it was not surprising that her list grew to a size beyond anything she had originally contemplated.

She dispatched the invitations to the post, through the offices of one of the footmen, and then sought out Pamela to inform her of how easy it had been to send out all the invitations, in one fell swoop.

Pamela was aghast to hear that almost fourscore of people would be descending upon them, the following week. If only her mother had let her know before she posted the invitations, she might have been able to winnow the list down to something reasonable. As it was, they were completely unprepared for such a crush, and would have to work day and night, buying the decorations and having them hung, shopping for food—food—food!!

"Oh, Mama, what have you done! How shall we ever be able to feed so large a group on this short notice? We shall have to get started at once! Galliard must be informed! Mama, what ever happened to the informal

212

dinner I suggested? How can we possibly do it all, and well? Our neighbors had never so many to come, and they had weeks to prepare! We have no time at all! Oh, Mama, and we wanted to make such a nice impression upon the Lyttons!" Pamela was close to tears.

Said Lady Pollworth: "I am sure you are making too much of it. I have an excellent sense for these things, and I feel that there is time enough. Now, do you go down to speak to the chef, and arrange for the repast. Remember, it is something very special that is required—and what with Mrs. Biggam to assist, it will go merrily along.

"But, before you go belowstairs, love, do speak to Gibbs and arrange with him for the decorations. I am sure you know what is needed. After all, we have seen how the neighbors have done up their houses. I am sure that we can do as well—but do it up better. You know how, and I shall be ready with advice, whenever you feel the need of it.

"Now then, do not forget to send to Geoffrey. Of course, he must be here—Oh dear, I do not recall if I included Kevin in the invitation to the Fairchilds. There's a dear! Do you inquire, tactfully, of course—Oh, but now I fear I am confused. Was it Kevin I omitted, or was it Margery—I never did care for her name—"

"Mama, Margery is a Dawlish. It had to be Eleanor you had forgot."

Lady Pollworth smiled thankfully. "You are so clever, my dear, to know whom I had forgot. It is a load off my mind, and I shall not have to worry about it further."

Pamela stared at her mother, unaware that her mouth had dropped open. "Mama," she began in a weak voice, "by any chance, did you remember

213

to include invitations to the Duke and Duchess of Pevensey?"

Lady Pollworth drew herself up in indignation. "Truly, Pamela, how can you doubt it? You know I have a perfect talent for this sort of thing!"

Miracle of miracles! It was minutes before the first guest could be expected to arrive, and for once, all four Pollworths, attired in their finest, were waiting with their eyes on the great clock in the hall. Lord Pollworth and Geoffrey were speaking together, while Lady Pollworth, with Pamela by her side, was standing proudly erect, a company smile already on her face. She looked bright and alert, and there was an air of accomplishment about her.

She turned to Pamela. "Dear, I wish you would stand straighter. See how proudly I do. When you consider the difference in our ages, and how much I have been through, getting everything all ready on such short notice, you, my pet, have no reason to slouch."

Pamela, who had been on the go steadily for the past week, achieving that very success her ladyship laid claim to, wished to sit down and wait. She was quite fatigued, and only now had she begun to think of Gerald and of his manner of mocking her. The thought of him added to her feeling of exhaustion. If she had dared, she would have begged to be excused, and gone to bed, pulling the covers over her head, until the affair was over.

Instead, she did as her mother bade her. She stood erect, and put a charming smile on her lips, just as a carriage was heard pulling to a halt in front of the house.

* * *

Hippolyte, with able assistance from Mrs. Biggam, had quite outdone himself. So said his Grace to Pamela, after the dinner was concluded, and the gentlemen came to join the ladies. He had singled Pamela out, and came right over to her.

"Thank you, Gerald. It is very kind of you to say so."

"Not at all!" he protested. "For my taste, there is not a better chef in all of London, than Hippolyte. I have missed his cooking dreadfully."

Pamela looked puzzled. "Is that why you were so anxious to be invited here? Just to taste of Hippolyte's cuisine, again?"

"I dare say it was a good part of the reason. We have had no great success in finding a replacement for him in the Pevensey kitchens. Ah, the quenelles d'houard! I would swear to it! He has done them better for you than he ever did them for me. Oh, and the ris de reau financière, devil take him! One of my special favorites—exquise!"

Pamela was content to see that he had been so pleased with the fare, but she did not particularly care for the excessively gastronomic quality of the compliments. She merely smiled pleasantly, and said: "I am sure I speak for the Pollworth family when I say I am happy your Grace has fared so well at our table."

A flicker passed over his face. "I say, am I beginning to bore you?"

"Not at all, your Grace. I enjoy your company and am honored that—"

"What is the matter with you, Pamela? Why have you suddenly gone so formal with me? Ah, I have it! You fear that I shall be asking for Hippolyte's services. You need have no worry on that score. I should not wish to interfere with your matrimonial plans—"

215

"Gerald, I thought you had said the last word about that—"

His eyebrows shot up. "Really? I do not see *why* you should think so. Consider that I have contributed, at some personal inconvenience, my chef to your cause, and you cannot fail to understand my continued interest. Has the dear fellow been of any assistance to you in your search for a husband?" he asked, his face falling into a set pattern of sobriety.

She felt not only put out, but hurt by his persistence. A tiny frown formed a little crease upon her brow as she replied: "Gerald, why do you go on in this fashion? It was a very silly thing I did. Of course, a chef, even if he were the finest in the land, would have nothing at all to do with it. I assure you, had I been in the market for a husband, I should have found him, whether there had been a chef in our kitchen or not."

His face broke into a smile. He reached out and brought her hand up to his lips. He did not release it, but said: "How marvelous! Then the joke is at my expense, for I thought that Hippolyte was most necessary to your plans. I pray then that I may have him back."

Still she could not convince herself that he was being serious. She studied him for a moment before she replied: "Just to prove that Hippolyte was not the least necessary to me, I should return him to you, upon the instant—but, as he was your gift to me, as I recall, I think I shall not. You would have to marry me to get him back into your kitchen—if I had anything to say to it."

"Is that a fact?!" he snapped.

"Yes, that *is* a fact," she retorted, feeling that for the first time she was getting her own back at him.

But it was not making her happy. In fact, she felt a distinct pain about her heart when, his eyebrows raised on high, he bowed to her and said: "We shall see about that!"

He wheeled about and stalked off. She watched to see where he was going, and saw him approach her father. She did not wait for her father to beckon to her. She had acted silly once again, and was experiencing an odd need to weep. She turned and went out of the chamber, in the other direction, finding her way to her mother's sitting room.

No one was there. She entered and sat down in an easy chair, resting her chin upon her hand, and began to contemplate how utterly ridiculous had been her behavior ever since she had first met Gerald.

It was Gerald's attitude towards her, she decided, that made her act so badly with him. He was always laughing at her. At this point, Galliard had nothing to do with it. True, the man was a positive culinary genius, but he was not essential to her contentment. What she had said to Gerald was the truth. A chef was not necessary to her, whatever her social ambitions might be.

These past weeks had gone to prove that the Pollworths, even without providing entertainment, were fully acceptable, and she herself had had nothing to complain about in that regard. Any one of a number of eligible gentlemen could have been in her pocket at her least sign of encouragement. But the one gentleman, whom she wanted above all others, could only talk chefs with her. All *he* wanted was his chef back.

As for her, he did not even wish to dance with her. She had convinced her mother not to sponsor a dance at this affair, thinking it might give her a chance to talk with Gerald. It had turned out exactly as she had hoped. He had spoken with her, but to what cordial purpose? None at all!

Maybe for all his attractive exterior, he was but a mere stick of a fellow, with a queer sense of humor. Unfortunately, at this point, it was over-late to discover that fact. She was sure that she was in love with him.

Oh, unhappy day! She was in love with a man so very high above her, and all he could think of was his horrid, old chef! Well, he did not have to worry! He could have the Frenchman back! Her father would see to it. Despite her brave retort, she knew all along that she did not have a word to say about it. The trouble was, what was she to do with herself? All the other gentlemen's company was palled, in comparison to brilliant Gerald!

It was enough to make a body weep—which she proceeded to do, and copiously.

Chapter XVII

It was about two hours later, and Pamela was still sitting by herself in the sitting room. She had heard the noise of departing guests a few moments ago, and now the house was quiet.

She stood up, dried her tears and put herself in order. As she turned towards the door, it opened and her father looked in on her.

"Ah, there you are, my dear. You look distressed. I dare say you have heard. The Duke of Pevensey has asked that Galliard be returned to him."

"Yes, Papa, I thought he would do so. He said as much to me. I am sorry to lose Hippolyte, but we still have Mrs. Biggam. I dare say we shall manage."

"I am very pleased to see you take that attitude, my child. Now, if you will present yourself in the library, his Grace awaits a final word with you."

"He is still here?"

"Yes, and I should not keep him waiting. Your mother is having to entertain her Grace in the meantime."

Pamela sighed. "Very well. I dare say he expects an apology from me. Very well, he shall have his apology."

"Apology? Daughter, what is going on? He never said anything of the sort to me."

"Another time I shall tell you all about it, Papa. Now, let us get this over with."

"Pamela, I bid you be respectful of his Grace. After all, he is a duke, you know."

"Yes, Papa, I know."

Pamela was disconcerted to find the duke smiling at her as she came into the library. She did not feel like smiling back. Instead, she thought to make the apology that was expected of her.

"Your Grace, I regret my language to you earlier, and would tender my humble apologies—"

"Here now, what is this business?" he exclaimed with a frown. "Are you so fickle? I thought we had a compact—but, if as you say, you regret it, devil take the apologies!"

"What compact? I recall no agreement between us. You demanded your chef back and I refused, though it was a silly thing to do. Papa has already informed me that Hippolyte is going back with you."

"Then he has misunderstood me. I thought I had made it plain. I would take him back, but only under the terms of our understanding, yours and mine. I say, you truly *have* forgotten them, haven't you?"

"Your Grace, I have not the faintest idea of any agreement. In fact, I was under the impression that all we ever do is to disagree."

"How can you say so, my dear, when all I have ever done is what you wished?"

Pamela stared at him, baffled and confused.

His Grace was looking uncomfortable. Suddenly, he did not appear to be so sure of himself. "Pamela, you did say to me that I could have Hippolyte back if I married you, did you not?"

There was an expression of incredulity on Pamela's face. Then it was quickly replaced with an indignant frown.

"Gerald, this is no time for another of your pranks. You know I could not have possibly meant it. Now, I wish you would go home!"

His answer caught her very much by surprise. He caught her in his arms, and brought his lips down to hers in a kiss that she had thought never to experience. Through all the shock of it, through all the passion of it, through all the glory of it, she was certain that it far exceeded anything she had imagined. Gerald loved her!!

"But Gerald, darling," Pamela inquired, many, many minutes after, "if you loved me from the first, why did you never court me, why did you never dance with me?"

"As long as it seemed that my chef had greater appeal for you than I did myself, I thought it wiser to wait a bit. I am rather pleased that you were finally able to make a distinction between us. In any case, I had to work it out, that I got the both of you. Can you imagine how it would have been? All the celebration of a marriage and I without a French chef?"

"There, you see? It *is* important to have a French chef. I was right from the first!" she taunted him, banteringly. "I got me a French chef and voilà! I am about to get me a husband!"

Gerald could barely kiss her for laughing so hard.

Finally, he eased her off his lap and said: "Your parents must be wondering what is going on with us. We had better go out to them."

Said Pamela: "Poor Papa, he has come to dote upon Hippolyte so."

"It is all right. He can take pride in the fact that he may be losing a chef, but he is gaining a son."

Needless to say, Lord and Lady Pollworth were both quite overcome at the news.

It took her ladyship a bit of time to accustom herself to the fact that she was to become mother-in-law to a duke, but she did manage. And she immediately began to make plans.

"Oh dear!" she exclaimed. "I have just finished with one affair and now I must see to another. But do not worry about a thing. I shall begin at once to prepare a list of guests. I am quite good at that sort of thing, you know, your Grace."

Thought Pamela to herself with a smile: Heavens! But it begins to appear it will be a long engagement!

Let COVENTRY Give You
A Little Old-Fashioned Romance

THE RUBY HEART   50112 $1.75
by Rebecca Danton

FASHION'S FROWN   50113 $1.75
by Georgina Grey

THE DEFIANT HEART   50121 $1.75
by Blanche Chenier

A CURIOUS COURTING   50115 $1.75
by Elizabeth Neff Walker

FAIR FATALITY   50116 $1.75
by Maggie MacKeever

REQUIEM FOR A RAKE   50117 $1.75
by Freda Michel

This offer expires 1 August 81   8082

Let COVENTRY Give You
A Little Old-Fashioned Romance

ROSE TRELAWNEY   50105 $1.75
by Joan Smith

COURTING   50107 $1.75
by Darrell Husted

DEBT OF LOVE   50108 $1.75
by Rachelle Edwards

REGENCY BALL   50109 $1.75
by Miriam Lynch

CHELSEA   50110 $1.75
by Nancy Fitzgerald

THE HALVERTON SCANDAL   50111 $1.75
by Helen Tucker

This offer expires 1 August 81   8092